REMEDY HOUSE

RUTH HAY

REMEDY HOUSE

BY RUTH HAY

Phase three in the Co-housing project:
Home Sweet Home

Can anything surpass their first year together in Harmony House?

One thing is certain. This amazing group of women has proved they are full of surprises.

But life is never perfect for long.

How the women deal with difficulties will test their friendships to the limit.

"Mavis and Hilary found us and brought us together. Vilma found her dogs. Eve found safety. Jannice found a career. Honor found a niece. And all of us found the unexpected; both good and bad."

CHAPTER 1

"Am I being paranoid? I expect you to tell me the truth. You know how much I respect your powers of observation."

The two women were settled on cushions on the bench at the back of the garden, now a bower of cream roses thanks to Mavis's efforts.

Hilary waited patiently for a response but her friend knew she had to carefully consider her words. She picked up the carafe of coffee and poured a second cup to give herself time to think.

Hilary looked out over the raised flower beds to the rear of Harmony House and tried to remember back over the eighteen months or so since six women had taken possession. How had matters come to this point so quickly? What had she missed in all the excitement of that first year? Certainly, there was much to take her attention. Furnishing rooms and establishing routines and making connections among diverse personalities was a task she had never presumed to be simple. Was she so absorbed in the financial details that she had ignored vital indicators?

One thing was clear to her now. It was time to take stock and Mavis Montgomery was the one who could best help with that.

"Don't dare blame yourself, Hilary! You know it was always possible that we entered this co-housing project with unrealistic expectations."

"Are you saying we have failed in some way?"

"Now, Hilary Dempster, that is not at all like you. Of course, we haven't failed! Just look around you and see the success we have achieved. Jannice has completed her training and is working as a Personal Support Carer, Honor is busier than ever with her financial investment clients, Eve is becoming an amazing artist, Vilma is delighted with the progress of her dogs and best of all, you have done wonders with Faith Jeffries; she is a triumph of hope over adversity. You have every reason to be proud. What on earth has brought you to this low point?"

Mavis looked carefully at her friend for the first time. Was there a sign of illness in the well-loved face? Was there a sign of aging? Neither of them was any younger and it could be said that the ups and down of the last year had taken a toll on both women. They were the senior members of the group, of course, but surely they were not *that* old? There should be decades of good health ahead.

Hilary was the prime mover in Harmony House. All looked to her for direction. What was this self-doubt about?

"I don't really know. It's just that I have this feeling of impending doom. Perhaps everything has gone *too* well and we have been tempting the Fates."

"But, there must be something concrete to get you thinking in such a negative way. What is it?"

Hilary looked upward and caught the flower head of a beautiful cream rose in her hand, pulling it to her nose and inhaling the delicious scent.

"These are the last roses of summer. There are a few signs of fall around us. I suppose I am a little afraid of what another winter will bring. Oh, I know the house is secure and warm and our finances are solid. We need not worry about the practical items. It's just the unknown that bothers me."

"Well, my dear, there's not much we can do about that, is there? Not one of us can predict the future.

Would you have imagined your struggles with Desmond could be resolved so speedily? He's well established in the new company position, and he's nearby, and seems to be grateful to his mother at long last. Take heart from that amazing turnaround."

"Yes, you are right, Mavis. As usual. I am worrying about nothing, I suppose.

Look, isn't that Vilma coming through the woods with the dogs? Please don't say a word to her or to anyone about our little talk."

Vilma Smith's early walk with her dogs was a time for contemplation. The woods were quiet. Birds ceased to chirp when the dogs arrived. The only sound was the burbling of the stream, their border marker. Astrid and Oscar rooted around happily, searching for the scent of squirrels. Treeing a squirrel was one of their delights. Vilma knew she could sit on a log and think in peace while they patrolled beneath a tree and watched until their prey got up the nerve to jump the distance to escape on the nearest branch of a further tree. She knew she could summon the dogs to her side with one whistle no matter the distraction. They were well trained now, thanks to Andy.

These days her thoughts were never far from Andy Patterson.

When she returned from the Jamaican beach

holiday at the end of February, they had reached a kind of border marker in their association, something similar to the stream beyond which the dogs were forbidden to go. She did not think of it as a relationship prior to that point. It was a student/ teacher association for mutual benefit. She got a superb dog trainer's advice and he got.............

Well, the truth was she did not known why he was keen to take on two rambunctious rescue animals. He could easily have dismissed her feeble efforts to restrain the dogs' temperaments. It was only after Jamaica that she heard the reason and she was still adjusting to that reality.

Andy Patterson was a survivor of a dreadful explosion that killed his police partner dog, King, and scarred his legs as well as his brain. The phrase he repeated whenever she questioned his monkish instincts to withdraw from society, was, 'I warned you about being a damaged man.'

She heard this several times and it had become a theme of his excuses. And yet, she saw signs of progress when she looked around the old farmhouse whenever they went inside for a cup of tea following the dogs' training sessions in the barn. It was the barometer of positive change as far as she was concerned. External change at least. She was not privy to his internal feelings, nor did she wish to be. She had given up on men.

The kitchen of the farmhouse now displayed a few touches of colour. Some arrived surreptitiously, accompanying the dogs while she was in Jamaica. Others, like the red kettle and matching toaster, she had insisted on as a gift to thank him. The set of red enamel mugs came later with the excuse that she could not pass on the great sale price. A stand of spoons with red handles was the last thing he was forced to accept and by then he was not at all pleased. She knew she could not push any further but it was a disgrace that he should be living in these sparse accommodations when he had marketable skills. She suspected he was punishing himself for the loss of King.

None of my business! I have truly sworn off men forever!

But, as long as Andy was willing to continue training her dogs for competitions, she was obliged to be in his company and that meant improving his living conditions for her own comfort at least. That was what she told herself but the more time she spent in 'Bleak House', the more she felt it was up to her as one of the few people he talked to in any depth. No, make that *only person* he talked to.

It was up to her to do something to help. It was

in her nature to try to make things better. It was how she coped with the unfairness of life. At Harmony House she found plenty of scope for this impulse to help, but most of her projects there had been fulfilled. Jannice was almost independent now she had a job and was about to take her driving test. She could still inject a little money here and there as needed from the seemingly endless source dear Nolan had left for her, but the house was running well and everyone was happy as far as she could tell. It was amazing, really, how six different women had blended into a supportive whole. Even the advent of the Teenager With Problems, as she always thought of Faith Jeffries, had not caused more than a ripple on the surface of their calm lives.

Of course, Hilary had taken on most of that burden with able assistance from Mavis. Vilma had little to do with the girl, after the November birthday fiasco, until the summer when she sat occasionally in the back seat while Jannice had preliminary driving lessons. Faith did not say much on these occasions. Vilma got the sense she was pretty tired from her summer job as packer in the grocery store checkout and the preparations her Aunt Honor was requiring before she took up grade ten courses at Saunders Secondary. As long as Faith caused no trouble with the dogs or their mistress, she was content to leave well enough alone.

Astrid's sudden yelp signalled the escape of the squirrel and the end of the early morning walk. Time to return home for breakfast and naps and a read through of the information Andy had supplied about the competition he wanted to enter the dogs in before the end of the year.

She passed Mavis and Hilary deep in conversation on the garden bench.

Probably discussing the next phase of garden development. Mavis is keen on an avenue of fruit trees.

It could take years before fruit would be produced but the trees could be a good screen from the nosy neighbour next door.

Honor Pace was enjoying a coffee break on the stone patio. She waved at Vilma as she passed and thought again that she was a woman of style and generosity. A woman Honor envied for those qualities, but she had learned from Mavis and Hilary to seek the positives in her own life and there were certainly many of those. First, was the fact she still had unchallenged access to the lower level of Harmony House. Of course the others were welcome to do laundry, rummage in their storage bins or simply enjoy the garden view from the patio. None of this disturbed her. In fact, after many years working alone in an apartment building, she relished the sound of human voices and was getting to know the other housemates through these contacts.

Her work was the second benefit as it was responsible for her ability to contribute to the monthly funds for herself and Faith. She was conscious that Faith had not purchased a share of the co-housing home and she meant to put aside a sum of money to compensate for this lack. Not a full share; just a portion representative of the number of years Faith would require to complete the first stage of her education. She completely agreed with Hilary that this was the way to future success and independence for her niece. Since her Faith had arrived, Honor had more motivation than ever before, to succeed in business and more clients had been the result.

The third item on her list was a personal one, related to her health. Taking a cue from Vilma she built regular exercise breaks into her work day and ventured into the woods behind the house where she found a clearing perfectly suitable for a stretch and twist yoga program she found on television.

Extra space inside her clothes was evidence this was having a good effect on her shape, but even better was the effect on her spirits. And it required plenty of strong self-talk to deal with Faith Joan Jeffries.

The girl was an expert manipulator when she wanted something. She knew her aunt had no previous experience with a female teenager. She also knew Honor had guilt attached to her feelings about an unknown niece who appeared out of the blue. The situation was rife for manipulation and Honor had to be constantly on her guard. Their relationship was much better when Honor set the rules.

They now had regular hours for homework help and that established a respectful manner. Faith sometimes erupted in frustration when she realized how far behind she was in her course content but Honor had a model in Hilary's teaching during the summer school months when Faith first appeared. Following that model she kept calm and gave the girl space to rant for a few minutes before pulling her attention back to the task in hand. It was one of many learning experiences with her niece.

High school courses had changed since Honor qualified in business technology. She could not really provide much help with advanced chemistry and physics but, fortunately, Jolene and Jarvis were able to coach Faith in after-school study group sessions at Jolene's house, leaving the internet-based courses for Honor to tackle.

On the one-to-one connection with Faith, however, things were moving slowly. Every now and then, Faith would reveal another incident from her life with Felicity. This was done to shock Honor and at first she was stunned to hear how her twin and Faith had managed to survive in the world with little money and fewer resources. She had no reason to disbelieve Faith even when her stories demonstrated a lack of moral conscience. Thieving from stores and taking flight from rental accommodation seemed to be normal for the pair and Honor always kept in the back of her mind that her niece might revert to these behaviours again if challenged enough. She knew Hilary would not entertain the idea of harbouring a thief in Harmony House.

The prospect of having to leave her comfortable life here, was a recurring nightmare for Honor. She could not abandon Faith to the world alone, ever again. If teenage chaos arrived to disrupt their existence, Honor would have no choice other than to recoup her investment and vacate Harmony House with Faith.

Vilma was cleaning the dogs' feet with the cloths and

towels she kept in the closet near the front doors when Eve stumbled on the stairs and almost fell into her arms. The dogs scattered in alarm and began to bark a warning. Vilma quickly hushed the dogs and pulled Eve upright again.

"Are you all right, Eve?"

"Oh, sorry! I lost my balance for a moment. The sunlight was in my eyes. I needed a breath of air. I haven't been sleeping well lately."

Vilma took a look and saw dark shadows under Eve's eyes. She seemed disoriented.

"Look, Eve! Give me a minute or two to settle the dogs and I'll join you on the porch. It's a fine morning. I'll bring us coffee and we can have a chat. Okay?"

Eve just nodded and stood there watching while Vilma cleared away the towels into a bin stored there for the purpose, then ran up the stairs with the dogs. She marvelled at the way Vilma seemed to handle everything with such confidence and style. Taking on two rambunctious dogs was not something Eve had ever aspired to do. In fact, when she compared her life to that of most of the inhabitants of Harmony House, she felt inadequate. The Kitchen Queen label was mostly a joke since the others were capable of producing good meals when they needed to. She did a little baking and kept the cupboards and fridge in order but others could take on those tasks if necessary.

She had grown to admire the ambition of that girl Faith who managed to keep up with school work, do some babysitting locally and still help with grocery shopping, even while working in the summer months. Of course, Faith was a teenager with all the energy in the world. Eve Barton's energy seemed to be fading with every month that passed. She had given up on painting. Her efforts were amateur and she feared comparison with the many talented artists residing in London.

Sighing deeply, she opened the front door and stepped out onto the porch. A breath of fresh air might help dispel the nightmares that were destroying her sleep of late. She plumped up the chair cushions on the wicker furniture and brushed a stray leaf off the table. Fall was approaching. Another long winter was coming. Last winter had been shortened by the fabulous week in the beach house in Jamaica but she could not count on that treat again. Hilary and Honor might want a chance to go there with Vilma.

She knew she should be doing something to earn money. She did not like seeing her inheritance deplete every month but her old skills in accounting were far behind those used currently and she did not have the confidence to start again, as Jannice had done, to acquire new marketable skills.

Another deep sigh escaped her lips but she managed to smile weakly when Vilma appeared with a tray of coffee mugs and two muffins on a plate.

"I found these in the warming oven. I don't know how you feel about eating your own baking, Eve, but these smelled so delicious I couldn't resist. You look as if a muffin or two would not do any harm. Have you lost weight?"

It was a personal question and Eve began to respond in the negative but Vilma's genuine look of concern made her stop and rethink. It was past time to let someone know how she really felt and Vilma Smith was not judgemental. She would listen.

"Yes. You are right. I am not eating properly and neither am I sleeping well. I hate to complain since I am so comfortable here and it seems a disgrace not to prosper in these surroundings. I have the peace I sought for so long but I don't seem to be able to enjoy it."

Vilma took a sip of coffee in an attempt to delay her response. She had not expected this confession from Eve. She really did not know her very well. Hilary and Mavis were the ones most involved in her story. She wondered why Eve had not gone to either of those capable women for help.

"I see I have embarrassed you, Vilma. Forgive me. A weak moment. Forget what I said."

"Well you surprised me for a moment, Eve, but I am not easily embarrassed and telling me how you feel is not a weakness. I think something is weighing on your mind and from what little I know of your life before Harmony House, I must say I am not at all shocked. Is it something new or is it back to the old fears related to your marriage?"

Eve broke off a piece of muffin and began to break it into tiny crumbs on the plate. This woman had gone right to the nub of the matter in seconds while she had been tossing and turning at night trying to work out what was happening.

"It started with my painting."

"But your paintings have been amazing, Eve. That Christmas card you made for me has pride of place in my room. How could such work lead to sleepless nights?"

"The paintings you have seen are fine. I used to enjoy doing them but there is another side to it and it comes out at night. I dream of scenes that are a million miles from Mavis's garden. These are dark and frightening, full of a menace I fear to name. In the daylight these dreams are now still haunting me and when I put brush or pencil to paper they return and seem to take over."

Vilma knew she was out of her depth. This was some kind of mental break-down and she was not capable of advising Eve. She could only give support and that she would do.

"Oh, Eve, how awful for you to have something you cherish turn into an attack. I am glad you told me about this although I don't have the knowledge to advise you. May I talk to Mavis on your behalf, or will you permit me to arrange a meeting with her? You don't need to reply immediately, of course. Let's just drink our coffee and enjoy the beautiful morning light."

She reached out her hand and held onto Eve's hand for a moment. There was nothing as soothing as the touch of a human hand. It conveyed so much more than mere human contact. It was something she had learned in her own life when Nolan held her hands, without a word said, until she calmed down.

Eve was unable to speak. She felt the warmth of Vilma's concern in both her words and her touch. A small portion of fear and worry dropped away and for a second or two she could believe there might possibly be a solution to her problem. She had not suspected when she woke this morning that help was so close at hand. Why had she not reached out before this?

She watched while Vilma consumed every crumb

of her muffin and was able to remember delight in simple things like providing pleasure for others through food. Perhaps this lovely morning was the start of her recovery and the lovely woman by her side was the means to that recovery. She berated herself for every unkind thought she had ever entertained about this rich woman with the fairy-tale life. No one who could feel so strongly for another person's pain could have sailed through life without learning compassion from her own disappointments and sorrows.

She picked up the mug and wrapped her hands around it. The aroma of fresh coffee reached her nostrils and she realized she had not been able to enjoy any food or drink for some weeks now.

A tear ran down her cheek but it was a tear of relief. She brushed it away before Vilma could notice.

It really was a beautiful morning. A new day in more ways than one.

CHAPTER 2

Jannice O'Connor jumped out of bed and immediately looked at her alarm clock.

Oh, Lord, I am so late!

Then she remembered. She had a day off and there was no need to rush around. She stretched and turned to admire the antique furniture surrounding her. The style and condition of the well-polished items was a constant reminder of how lucky she had been to meet these wonderful women who enriched her life in so many ways they were simply uncountable.

Her decades of struggle in the mean little terraced home in Old East London were fading. This was her new reality and with it came new friends, new work opportunities and soon, a car in which to further expand her horizons. Each week she put away money to purchase her first vehicle and as the sum grew, so did her confidence in her abilities.

On the walls of her room she had the framed prints of herself wearing the beautiful, fragile, wedding trousseau garments found in the old home's attic. These had provided the sum of money, added to the house sale, allowing her to secure a place at Harmony House.

She cherished the women, especially Vilma, who had opened her eyes to so many possibilities.

She cherished her immaculate room devoid of clutter and dust and debris from years of former inhabitants. Everything here was pristine from the kitchen to the basement office where Honor held sway. Every few days, Jannice swept around the common areas with dusters and vacuum cleaners but it was no imposition. Each woman felt as house-proud as she did and there was seldom anything major to do. Of course, Vilma took full responsibility for her dogs and made sure there were no signs of their existence indoors or out.

Jannice had one or two concerns about the girl, however. Once or twice when Faith left the door to her room open, Jannice saw a tangle of bedclothes with shoes and books scattered over the carpet. She suspected this was typical teen behaviour but she had never had a sister or brother to judge by and it was not her business to draw attention to the matter. She had better things to do with her limited spare time. Honor should take care of her niece.

When she had a few moments alone, she would fire up the tablet Vilma had loaned her and check in on Mitchell Delaney. When they met in Jamaica she never suspected he was genuinely interested in her tales of Irish ancestors and the trousseau in the attic, but since February he had persisted in contacting her with questions about her life story.

It seemed he really was an author. She found him on Google. The idea that he wanted to write about her was something she doubted from the first. Now he was asking if they could meet in Quebec City over Christmas so as to record some interviews and prepare an outline for his publisher.

She had never ventured out of Ontario but he said he would cover all the costs and set her up in a hotel for the stay. She tucked this information close to her chest and thought about it from time to time. She had not yet responded to the request. She would discuss it with Vilma first, of course, but for now it was her own little secret and she loved the way it made her feel so special.

Sure now, it's a miracle that the old stories I heard on my Ma's knee are causing this lovely man to be interested.

Not that it's in any way a personal interest. No! No! It's about a book he wants to write. But lovely to think anyone cares that much. Who would have believed this could happen to Jannice O'Connor?

Faith Joan Jeffries, known at school as J.J., was a person with two lives. In one she was the good student who did her homework and kept up with the expectations of Harmony House's residents.

In the other she reverted to the girl she used to be while living hand-to-mouth with an addicted mother and never knowing what the next knock at the door would bring. Not that she really wanted to be that old Faith. It had been a difficult time, especially when her mother overdosed and landed in hospital leaving her daughter to survive on her own.

But all that was behind her now and she did appreciate the comfort and support of a house full of mature, sensible women who arranged regular meals and would do anything to help her.

There were times, however, when all that became a trifle cloying. Even Aunt Honor could be too much sometimes, despite good intentions. The truth neither of them really knew how to be in a relationship that had appeared out of the blue one day. It was difficult for each of them. It might never become really comfortable. Faith shrugged off these thoughts. By the time she could apply for a scholarship and gained some qualifications she would not need the Harmony House mothering.

She would be free.

And yet, there was a part of her that was afraid of that freedom. Who would she be, once she left Honor behind, with no family in all the world? How much did she care?

The discussions about this dilemma took place in Jolene's house in Westmount where Faith, Jessica and Jarvis met twice weekly during the summer for what was termed a 'study group'. Jolene's mother was cool. She provided snacks and drinks but left the foursome on their own in the basement rec room with the weekly caution, 'No nonsense now!'

Actually their deliberations were anything but nonsense. The J.J. group took very seriously Faith's situation.

"You'd be out on your own in some college dorm anywhere you wanted. Sounds like heaven to me!"

"That's because you have always had family to rely on when things are tough. It's different when you have no one."

"Do you mean your Aunt Honor would be out of your life?"

"Probably! Let's face it, she was practically forced

to take me on and she has no experience whatsoever with a teenager. She left home as soon as she could. I don't see her standing in my way."

"But what about your father?"

Jarvis's questions caused a chill to fall on the room and its inhabitants. Jolene reached over and gave him a hard punch on his arm, saying "Dimwit! You know Faith doesn't have a father."

"Back off, Jo! Biologically speaking, *everyone* has a father."

"Give him a break, Jolene. He's right. If my mother had ever told me who my real father was, I would definitely look him up. He could be rich for all I know. But that horse died years ago. I have no clue."

Jessica, who had been listening to this exchange in a thoughtful way, piped up with another angle.

"What about the man who married your mother, that Jeffries guy whose last name you have, so she could have a place to live when you were born?"

"What about him?"

"Well, he might know something about Felicity's life when she was a teen. Didn't you say he was a bit of a wild one too? He might know the whole gang of them."

This was a new thought. Glances were exchanged around the group as the impact of the idea grew. It was a possibility Faith had never considered.

"But how would I even find him? He left while I was still a little kid."

This was the kind of project the 'study group' preferred to boring old science. They quickly got on board.

"Do you have a photo of him?"

"Do you remember his name?"

"Did your Mom keep a diary?"

"Do you have any paper records that could help?"

Faith just looked around at her friends with an amused expression on her face. Finally she shot off a response to their questions.

"No. No. No. And no. You guys have no idea what my life was like. When you leave in the middle of the night nothing extra can be carried along. My Mom regularly burned paperwork so there was no paper trail to follow. I never saw photos like other people have. Remember, she did not even tell me she had a twin sister!"

"Oh! *Right*."

Seconds ticked by while the impact of Faith's comments sunk in. Not one of her listeners had an early life like the one their pal had just described. It was a shame.

"We can't give up this easily, gang. Think outside the box. There has to be a way."

Jarvis sounded positive but the others were not seeing a choice until Jolene jumped up from the sofa and almost spilled her drink all over the floor.

"Wait a minute! We have the resources of the entire internet at our fingertips. People go online and find family members all the time. I know this situation will be more difficult but let's give it a try. What could it hurt?"

Jessica, who was the level-headed one, was not about to let that challenge pass without comment.

"Hold up there! You know better, Jo. Anyone could pretend to be who J.J. wants and be only looking for money or for something worse."

"We know all about internet trolls and creeps. Haven't we had endless warnings about all that in school? J.J. wouldn't be all on her own in this. We would be watching from the sidelines and checking everything for hoaxes and stuff."

"Excuse me! Stop right there! You guys are assuming I want to find this man who deposited his sperm and left my mother to cope with the results. Why would he even care about an unknown daughter? He has never made any attempt to find me or my Mom. Why should he? It was likely a one-night stand."

"You can't know that J.J. Maybe he's out there looking for a son or daughter and longing to find you."

"That's a fairy tale, Jo. Not reality. It would be a complete waste of time.

Now, who's going to explain this fractal image to me?"

She pushed the neglected study book to the front of the table and raised her eyebrows signalling the personal discussion was over as far as she was concerned.

Faith had firmly dismissed the subject but Jolene was not going to let it die down that easily. *That's not what real friends do,* was echoing in her mind.

Mavis Montgomery often left the door to her main floor tower room open just enough to let Marble slip in or out. Although the cat had freedom to go outside she did not seem to want to do that very often. Mavis thought she could smell the dogs and was afraid of them, or it might be that Marble was getting older and less able to adjust to all the different people moving about in Harmony House at all hours of the day. She still spent time sleeping under Mavis's piano in Faith's room. It was only a few steps away and during term time, Faith was gone for most of the day. The girl did not seem to mind having a cat there.

It had been a mutually satisfactory solution until recently. For some reason, Marble had begun to make a nest on the bottom shelf of Mavis's book cases. These shelves were left clear since bending down that far to read labels on CD cases or books was not easy for Mavis to do. Marble had taken over the space and she began to lay soft items there. At first, Mavis had not noticed, but when she almost tripped over a red sock one morning, she looked more carefully and saw the sock was only one of several soft items that did not belong to the cat's owner. There were two large elastic head bands and a blue undershirt with a hole in the bottom edge that must belong to Faith. She began to wonder why the girl had not complained about missing items and that made her wonder what condition the former guest suite was now in. Mavis presumed Faith was taking care of things independently as were all the other residents of Harmony House. It now occurred to her that, unlike the others, Faith was still a child with a child's habits.

She decided to take a peek inside Faith's domain at the first opportunity. She would retrieve the lost items and replace them with a spare cushion cover for Marble's comfort. If she should be caught on her mission of inspection, she would have the sock and the other items with her to provide an excuse.

The opportunity arose the next day.

Faith had gone into town to shop for new clothes for school. She was meeting up with her friends for lunch and a look around the City Centre Mall where stores for younger people were clustered. She would be gone for most of the day.

Mavis did not want to be seen spying, so she waited until the house was quiet in the late afternoon. Vilma was off with the dogs at Andy's. Jannice was working on updating her professional papers, and Eve was baking in the kitchen. Honor was safely downstairs as usual, and Hilary was resting, which was something Mavis had recommended.

She crept along the hallway to Faith's room, closely followed by Marble who seemed to feel she was needed on this mission. The guest suite had no door lock as privacy was something everyone in the house respected. Mavis felt a flash of guilt as she pushed open the door and went inside. She soothed her conscience with the reminder that she was only looking. She would not touch a thing. Whatever she discovered would be Honor's problem, not hers.

The bed was the first thing she saw. The bedclothes were piled to one side as if left there when Faith jumped out of bed in the morning. On the mattress were two sets of headphones and a pen with an open notebook or diary filled with handwriting. She deliberately turned her head so as not to read Faith's writing. It was likely a good thing the girl had an outlet for her thoughts and concerns but those were private.

From the bed a trail of underwear led to the closets, open and very disorganized and onward to the bathroom, the floor of which was concealed by a layer of wet towels and discarded T-shirts. Long strands of pale fair hair clumped in the sink and the hairbrush was in the shower, together with a toothbrush and toothpaste. Obviously the shower was used for multiple purposes to save time in the morning. Mavis doubted the sink would drain much longer with all the hair left there.

She did not proceed any further. She had seen enough. No wonder Marble felt free to steal from the room. Faith could not have noticed a few things missing in this total mess. The condition of the room offended Mavis's house-proud nature. The six women had gladly taken in this strange child and she must understand her responsibilities as a result of their generosity.

She would hold onto the stolen items and use them as an introduction to the topic when talking with Honor during their morning coffee break. No one need know she had been so intrusive. She had not looked specifically at the carpet in the former guest suite but she was glad they had decided to cover parts of it with patterned rugs.

Goodness knows what such carelessness will do to a pure white carpet not to mention the possibility of mould in the bathroom? Something needs to be done about this. Right away.

CHAPTER 3

Vilma had been driving the long straight road to the turn-off to Andy Patterson's farm for months now. She could have driven it blindfolded, she supposed. She certainly allowed her mind to drift as she drove. The dogs were used to the routine and slept quietly in the back of the car. During the summer months and into the Fall when Andy's gardening business was in full swing, the training sessions were mostly in the early evenings. Vilma had seen how tired Andy was after a day of physical labour and she would pick up chicken wings or a bowl of chilli to heat up in the small oven in the farm kitchen while Andy put the dogs through their paces. She hoped to add a small microwave to the meagre kitchen implements at Christmas to make this task easier.

The training arena in the big barn had been expanded to take up more than the original space and the challenges Andy supplied had also expanded in complexity. It was a marvel to Vilma that her dogs could figure out how to negotiate a puzzle tunnel or turn and change directions on the mere movement of Andy's hand as a guide. Astrid and Oscar loved the exercise and their behaviour overall, improved with every session in the barn. Vilma now had the confidence to take them anywhere with her. She knew they were obedient to her commands as well as those of their 'master'.

The big challenge ahead did not faze the dogs. They took everything in their stride, but for Vilma it was a stage in the training that would require her to go out of town with Andy to the convention site near Cornwall, Ontario. She had thought this over and toyed with the idea of leaving the dogs and her car to Andy for the two day competition but she was not comfortable with this idea and she really did want to see how they coped in such different circumstances than the barn.

Andy had introduced a recording of loudspeaker announcements and the crowd background noises of a busy arena to accustom the dogs to the competition conditions. The dogs were fine with it. Vilma got very nervous imagining the challenges ahead and often left to go to the peace of the riverside where a long-legged grey heron often stood like a sentinel in the middle of the stream watching for passing fish to spear on his beak.

She could relate to the heron. She, too, was watchful and thoughtful. Such patience was not in her nature, however, and she was growing impatient with herself.

What is it I want? What more could I need? I have a perfect living situation at Harmony House.

The other women are amazing. There is always something going on but no one interferes with another person's privacy and yet help is at hand should it be required. It's exactly what Hilary and Mavis hoped for. It's exactly what I hoped for, so what is this restlessness about?

Neither the silent heron nor the river provided an answer to this question but the gentle breeze in the willow branches was soothing to her spirit and she plopped down on the grassy bank and absorbed the peace in solitude. In a few minutes she would go into the farmhouse and heat up the pasta dish she had brought with her. In a cooler in the car she had a packet of cooked shrimp to add to the meal. Perhaps she would save a shrimp or two for the heron.

Andy Patterson found great satisfaction working with Vilma's dogs. He was glad to see them but he knew he was not yet ready to have a dog of his own. The memory of King was still too raw to consider that possibility. And yet, the thought of the coming winter was crouching on the border of his mind.

The first outing with the dogs to a trial competition would see him through the fall but the cold, lonely months ahead were the most difficult of the year for him. Last winter Vilma had regularly brought the dogs to him for weekly training. There was no telling how severe this winter would be. He could be isolated for weeks on end if the snowfall was extreme. He knew he had made good mental progress thanks to Vilma's generosity in sharing her dogs with him. That progress was hard-won and he dared not slip back into the dangerous depression of the years following the accident.

He turned his attention back to the training circuit and considered adding another foot in height to the climbing obstacle. Astrid could easily do it and Oscar always followed her without question.

He had sent away for the entry forms for the competition and looked on the website for an idea of the challenges.

The dogs were more than ready in his estimation. September should bring them to the peak of condition and in October he would increase the practice sessions to equip them for any unexpected challenges the competition might present.

He had considered asking their owner for permission to take the dogs by himself. He suspected Vilma was not likely to agree. They had never been away from her except for the week in February when he had taken care of them while she was in Jamaica. It was not likely she would want to miss the event to which so much time and training had been devoted. So it was to be the two of them in a hotel somewhere. He felt uncomfortable about this and searched his mind for a reason. Vilma had never stepped over the line of privacy he had drawn. It was his unplanned confession about King and the circumstances of the accident that had given her the chance to do so. To his relief, all had resumed normal communication after that possible breach.

The nearest she had come to a female reaction was when he appeared out of the snow at London airport to rescue the four women from Harmony House on their return to Canada from their holiday in February. Since then there had been nothing overtly personal between them. Even when he objected to the gifts she insisted on bringing to 'brighten up his life', she accepted his criticism and continued to be calm and consistent with him. In his experience of women this was unusual. His former wife would have thrown things at him for his ungrateful comments and promptly taken the offending items away forever. Of course, Vilma Smith was not like other women of his acquaintance. Truth was he could not quite figure her out. She was smart and stylish; so much so, that he often noticed the contrast between his country farmhouse existence and the appearance of this obviously town-raised woman of the world.

He concluded she had to have money. No one living in such accommodation as Harmony House was short of cash, yet she never displayed any overt disdain for his simple way of living. She wanted to add to his kitchen supplies, which he thought was a typical female reaction, but she backed down when he indicated she was beginning to invade his space.

She was different all right. It was perplexing. Vilma Smith was beginning to occupy a considerable part of his thinking. She was an enigma, a distraction. As long as she stayed on the border of his life, that distraction had benefits.

The barn door was open and the smell of food drifted in from the kitchen. He looked down at his feet where Oscar and Astrid were sitting with tongues lolling out waiting for his next command. He had missed the last section of their round because of his distracted thinking about Vilma. There was something comforting in the thought that she was waiting for him, and for her dogs. There was also a modicum of comfort in the fact she was one of the few people who knew about King and the resultant burns to his legs. And she had not flinched when he reminded her how damaged he was.

Vilma Smith was different from any other women he had encountered. That was for sure.

"Let's go, you two! Something good is waiting."

On training days, Vilma eliminated a last run of the day for her dogs since they had a complete workout with Andy as well as a good feed of kibble afterwards. She had shared the pasta meal with him and was now ready to retire to her room and spaz out with something absorbing from Netflix.

There was, however, one thing niggling at the back of her mind still to be done. She had not had the chance to talk to Mavis about her conversation with Eve. She took the dogs into her room and settled them, planning to unload her concern onto the capable shoulders of Mavis and return to her evening diversions with a clear mind.

She tapped gently on Mavis's door and was told to come inside where she found Mavis and Hilary seated side by side on the couch and deep in conversation.

"Oh, excuse me ladies. I did not want to interrupt you. I can talk to you tomorrow, Mavis."

Hilary stood up and shook her head.

"No, Vilma. I am glad to see you. We need your input about something. Please sit here with me. Mavis will be comfortable on the bench at the end of the bed.

"Are you sure? You look like it's a serious conversation."

"Well we do get together every so often to discuss the state of the world and the temperature of Harmony House. Your opinion is always welcome, Vilma."

"If you are sure? I have a matter to discuss that fits into your agenda, I believe. If I may, I'll deal with it now and leave you in peace?"

"Go ahead," said Mavis, with a sidelong glance at Hilary. It was uncommon for Vilma to need any help.

With her extensive resources and creative nature she was ingenious at solving problems on her own.

"Right, I'll get straight to the point. I talked to Eve the other day and I am concerned about her mental and physical state. Of course, I am no expert and I thought at once of you, Mavis, as the person most likely to know how to help Eve."

"What exactly did you feel was wrong?"

"She confessed to not eating or sleeping well and she mentioned bad nightmares that were stopping her from enjoying her painting."

Hilary reached out and patted Vilma's hand. "You will not be surprised to hear we have just been sharing similar concerns about Eve. Mavis has promised to talk to Eve and see what can be done for her. As you know they went through a traumatic event together."

"I am relieved to hear you will help her. If I can do anything you will let me know?"

"Don't rush off yet, Vilma. There's something else we could use your advice about."

Vilma settled back down in the chair. She had such confidence in these two women who were responsible for the whole co-housing experiment. She couldn't imagine what they could possibly want her advice about.

Mavis took over. "It's a delicate matter about Faith. I had a glimpse into her room recently and it's in a terrible condition, so much so that it may take a plumber and a carpet cleaner to sort it out."

"I have very little to do with Faith. My contacts

with teenagers have not been positive in the past. How could I help?"

"Oh, it's just a matter of how to approach Honor. We feel she should be the one to tackle this. The fact is, I infringed on Faith's privacy by entering her room without permission and I am reluctant to admit this to Honor."

Vilma now saw the dilemma. She also saw her peaceful evening with Netflix vanishing.

"I'm sure you meant no harm by going into Faith's room. As it happens, I have seen something of the mess in there. Sometimes when she goes off early for the bus she has left the door ajar. I have closed it for her to stop the dogs from wandering in where they are not wanted. I know that would be upsetting to Marble."

"That's very thoughtful of you, Vilma, and you have just solved the problem for me."

"How did I do that, Mavis?"

"Well, if you are willing to tell Honor what you just told us, the matter will be in her hands without a lie having to be told. May I ask you to do this for me?"

Vilma realized she was not going to escape this responsibility. No one who knew Mavis's kind nature could ever refuse a request from her. She was always looking out for the residents of Harmony House.

"I guess it's a fair exchange, Mavis. If you will help out Eve, I will talk to Honor about what I saw."

"That's what I call a good conclusion. Thank you, Vilma. We can always count on you for support.

By the way, I've been meaning to tell you how much I appreciate having guard dogs in the house. If Mavis and Eve and I had had a dog at Camden Corners perhaps what traumatized Eve could have been prevented."

Mavis made note of what Hilary said and decided to make Eve aware of that factor in her current safety.

Vilma made her exit and decided there was no time like the present to tackle Honor. The dogs were asleep and the evening was almost over in any case. She knew Honor worked late. A couple of minutes and she would be shot of the whole thing.

Honor Pace was just coming to the end of a complex piece of investing structure for a new business client. It involved providing copies of market results for Standard and Poor companies over the past six months. The recommendation was solid and as soon as the clients saw the breakdown they would be satisfied that she knew what she was doing.

She was checking the Asian exchange markets before closing her computer for the day when she heard a polite tap at the door leading from the covered deck. She got up at once and stood for a moment to stretch and get her balance before ascending the steps and sliding the bolt along.

"It's just me, Honor. I won't take much of your time, I promise."

"Vilma! I don't see much of you these days. Please come inside. Can I get you a cup of tea or coffee?

I am about to have my last snack before bed."

"That sounds very nice. I'll have tea, thanks. Milk no sugar."

The tea ceremony would give Vilma the chance to get oriented to Honor's little kingdom in the lower level. She had not been here since the rescue mission on the day of Faith's fifteenth birthday. On that occasion the floor was cleared to allow for party food and music to take precedence. Now it looked like a proper office environment with a substantial L-shaped desk on wheels and cabinets for documents and files. Honor's private space was to the rear facing the bank of folding windows that led onto the stone patio and the garden. Mavis had installed solar lanterns on the main path and they were lit up like small jewels in the darkness.

"It's really nice here with that open view, Honor."

"I am well aware how lucky I am to have this space for my work. It's a perfect environment and I would be happy to interview clients here if that ever became necessary. The only thing it lacks is sufficient room for another bedroom for Faith. I feel badly that no one can invite a guest while she is in the suite set apart for that purpose."

"I wouldn't worry about that, Honor. Most of us have no need of visitor accommodations but your comment does bring up the reason for my interruption this evening."

"You are more than welcome here, Vilma, at any time. I presumed you might need investment advice but it sounds like you have something else on your mind?"

Vilma assembled her thoughts while watching Honor wheel a table into position for the tea things. She noted how much more mobile Honor was and how much younger she looked now she had dropped some of the weight accumulated after her hip problem. For the first time she also noticed a resemblance between Faith and her aunt. Take away the red hair and they were of a similar height and shape of face.

She could benefit from some more flattering clothing to fit her new shape. I'll keep that in mind when I do my next closet upgrade.

"I don't want to appear to be prying, Honor, but I think you should know the state of the guest suite has deteriorated since Faith took possession. Now, I can see from your expression that this is news to you. I want you to know I accidently saw inside her room when she left the door open. That's all I have to say on the matter. I will leave it up to you what you do next."

"Oh, I had no idea! I thought it best to give her some privacy. She has been very busy with school and studying and her part-time job as well as the babysitting for our neighbour on the crescent. I never gave a thought to housekeeping issues. That's my fault, Vilma, and I am grateful you brought it to my attention."

"Don't beat yourself up about this, Honor. You also have a lot to cope with. From what I've heard, Faith's childhood did not leave much time for learning how to do housework. I'm sure you two can sort this out together in no time.

Now let's talk of something else while I drink this delicious brew here, then I must get back to my charges. One more trip to the woods should ensure a quiet night for me."

"I must say, I admire the way you have coped with the dogs, Vilma. I wish I had done as well with my niece. It's been a sharp learning curve for me. Whenever I feel I am getting a grip on teen thought, something else happens to set me back on my heels again. She's so different from me. My own experience as a teenager could not be more different."

"You have to get credit for her progress, Honor. She has come a long way as regards her education and she is independent in many ways. She behaved beautifully while I was giving Jannice driving lessons. It's good for her to have goals in life. She sees that in you, of course."

"Thanks for the encouragement. I need to be more alert with Faith. She has her mother's influence to fight against all the time."

"That's what I mean. Give her credit whenever you can. If I can help, let me know."

"You have helped already, Vilma. Thanks again."

"No problem. Good night, then."

CHAPTER 4

Leonard Harper's surgery was on a short, quiet, leafy street downtown leading to the Thames River Park. It had once been his family home and was now exclusively his office and residence. He kept the two functions as separate as possible. Even his trusty secretary and mistress of the office staff, Barb, never entered the top level where his private quarters were. His living room had a small balcony from which he could see through the trees to the green space that bordered the river. On the more stressful days he sat here with the once-weekly cigar that was all he permitted himself, and dreamt of sailing away on the Thames far from London and the ills of his many patients. It was only a dream. His life of service was here where he had always been.

Here he would die and be buried in the churchyard beside his mother and father.

Leonard rarely gave a thought to life after doctoring. His father had soldiered on into his eighties and expired only a few years after retiring. It was the family pattern and he saw no reason to diverge from that. His practice was still busy, although these days he had more elder patients than young ones. Most had stayed with him through the years in the knowledge that he not only understood their ailments, he often knew their parent's generation's problems as well.

Hilary Dempster was one of these. Leonard had seen her husband Mark through his last illness and advised their son Desmond on a few health issues on his infrequent trips home from Toronto. Hilary was seldom in his surgery which he put down to a very active and satisfying professional life in education.

He was, therefore, surprised to see her recently and the reason for her appointment had lingered in his mind far more than normally.

She came right to the matter in hand as soon as he entered the examining room.

"I don't want to waste your time, Leonard. Do you have any tests for Alzheimer disease?"

He was immediately shocked and had difficulty concealing it from her. Hilary Dempster was one of the most sensible and intelligent women he knew. Such a request was highly unlikely coming from her.

He looked with his physician's eye at her appearance and attitude to see if there were any clues to explain her question. Of course, it was possible she was asking on behalf of another person.

He could see nothing untoward in her appearance. She was smartly dressed as usual, and her greying hair was neatly combed in a flattering style. Her hands, clutching a black leather purse on her knees, were as elegant and well-tended as ever, with clean, unpolished nails. He always found hands and nails to be prime indicators of women's health. The only thing to note about her was an impatient tapping of her right foot on the tile floor.

"Why on earth do you want to know about Alzheimer disease, Hilary?"

"Leonard, we have known each other for many years. I have come to you because I am worried about my mental state and I need to know if I am in trouble."

His analytical mind had taken over at that point and he asked for a list of her 'symptoms' with little expectation she was a candidate for the disabling disease.

All she could supply were the forgetfulness and occasional confusion that are the inevitable companions to aging. He tried to reassure her with tales of his own inability to find his car keys and the time he put the milk back in a cupboard instead of the fridge, but she cut him off abruptly.

"I have always been able to rely on a fully-functioning brain, Leonard. I am not stupid, nor am I subject to hallucinations. When I state that I have observed considerable changes in the functioning of my mental powers, you must believe me. It could be the beginning of dementia. I am prepared to concede that much. Were it not for my current responsibilities, I would not be overly concerned, but I have taken on the welfare of five, no six, other women and I cannot jeopardize their futures."

Now it became clear that Hilary Dempster was thinking mainly of others. He vaguely remembered Barb saying something about a special housing co-op that Mrs. Dempster was involved in. She was likely overburdened and expecting too much of herself. This was a common problem with conscientious females of a certain age. He offered to give her a written test she could do at home and an experimental blood test with the proviso that no results were guaranteed. She accepted these eagerly. Then he moved on to the more probable cause of her distress.

"When was the last time you took a break,

Hilary? The responsibility for others can be overwhelming at times. I am going to suggest something unusual to you but hear me out. I believe you need to get away from your responsibilities and find a cause to which you can devote a few hours a week."

She was offended.

"You mean *volunteering*? The last thing I need is *more* work!"

"I imagine you would not respond positively if I told you to take a holiday. Am I right?"

She knew he was right.

"Doing something different will allow you to refocus your energy and restore your confidence in your mental powers, which, I may say, Hilary, are as formidable as they have always been. I will take a blood sample if you insist.

Please make an appointment with Barb for one month from now and seriously consider what I advised.

Now, get yourself out of my office and buy an ice cream on the way home."

Hilary did as ordered, but she was stunned by Leonard's conclusion. He did not think she was an obvious Alzheimer victim. He recommended getting out into the community in some way; a thought she had never before entertained but would now start to consider. She also remembered his comment about a holiday and it came to her mind that, if Vilma wished to offer her Jamaican beach cottages again, she might just take the opportunity. From what Mavis had said, it was the perfect get-away spot.

Feeling much relieved, she stopped by an ice cream stand and sat eating a huge cornet watching the crowd go by and thinking it was an absolute age since she had the leisure to sit and do nothing.

Perhaps Leonard Harper's assessment was more accurate than she would ever have suspected.

CHAPTER 5

"Hey, J.J. It's Jolene! I've had a brilliant idea."

"Oh, do tell."

"You know that major assignment for Grade 10 Computer studies?"

"Yes. Don't tell me you've done it already?"

"No. But I have an idea for *your* project."

"Why do I think this is going to be bad news for me?"

"I can't imagine why. This is a guaranteed A+ and you can get started on it before school. You know we are supposed to arrive with an idea planned out in detail for the first class?"

"All right, I suppose. What's involved?"

"It's simple. The project is to find out about your father by using online sources."

"Now, wait just one minute, Jo! You know I said that's impossible. I can't even start. I haven't a single bit of information to help me. "

"I had an idea about that. Just ask your aunt what she remembers. All you need is a name or two and we can go from there. I am thinking you could start a blog about the process. There must be heaps of kids out there who are looking for family for one reason or another. It's a major identity thing with families and don't forget about the health issue. What if your father has some health problem that you could prevent for yourself, if you only knew about it?"

Faith was momentarily struck dumb. She knew Jolene was a major brain at school but this amount of involvement in a friend's life was something foreign in her experience. No one of her own age had ever reached out to help Faith Jeffries. Had she not know the girl for some time now she would naturally assume there was something to be gained for Jolene in this wild scheme. Was it even possible Jo just wanted to be a good friend?"

"I don't know what to say, Jo. This is huge. You make some great points. I hope you've done as much work on your own assignment and not wasted too much time on this."

"It's up to you to decide if I've wasted time. As far

as I'm concerned, I think you should do it. If there's nothing else of interest in grade ten, at least you would have some answers to questions about your identity."

"You mean *if* I decide to do this."

"Yeah, sure! It's your call J.J."

"I'll think about it, that's all I can say right now."

"Good enough. Are you keeping the new clothes you bought downtown?"

"I might return the skirt and I'm not certain about the boots."

"Well, make up your mind soon. We need to coordinate outfits for the first day back in September."

"Okay. And, Jo............ Thanks."

"See you soon, kid! Don't forget to let me know your decision. We need to get going on this."

Faith plopped down on her bed and pulled the cover over her. She felt chilled although it was a pleasant temperature in her room. The thought of delving into her past life brought up memories and regrets about her Mom; memories she had tried to bury deep. Mavis had given her the speech about the stages of grief and how they could not be avoided, but it seemed easier to submerge all that in her new life in London where every single thing was diametrically opposite to all she had known in her travels with her mother. Safer to let sleeping dogs lie.

Safer not to dig too deep.

And yet, Jolene brought up some important points.

What if her father had already died from some dread disease that would pop up and ruin her life one day?

What if her father was alive somewhere and wondering what had happened to his child?

What if he never cared about her and never wanted to know and just refused any requests?

That's the most likely scenario! Didn't Honor say he took off as soon as he knew my Mom was pregnant?

He was a loser. Who wants a loser for a father? Better not to know him at all.

She was beginning to feel satisfied with this conclusion until another set of thoughts popped up.

What if he is married without children and I am the only one he will ever have?

What if he is married with several children who are my step brothers and sisters?

Brothers and sisters? Me?

Stop this, Faith Joan Jeffries! They call it idle speculation. It's a waste of time like I said before. Enough already!

She grabbed up her earbuds and started a music

app on her phone, turning the volume up as high as she could tolerate to blast the foolish thoughts out of her head.

∾

Honor Pace did not want to challenge her niece on the topic of housekeeping but the more she postponed the inevitable discussion, the more it got in the way of her work. Finally she connected by phone with Faith and asked her to come for a talk.

"Uh, what's the talk about? I am heading downtown to meet the kids from school. There's a free rock concert in Victoria Park."

"That's fine. Stop by when you get back and don't be too late. If it's after dark, call from the bus stop and one of us will pick you up."

Honor cringed when the words left her mouth. *That sounded like typical Mom talk, something I have no right to. I can't be over protective with Faith but how does an aunt behave? Are there online courses for this situation?*

She fully expected to be ignored. So, later in the evening when she was about to check upstairs to see if Faith had already returned home, she was not too surprised to get an angry phone call from her niece.

"What's going on here? Someone has been nosing around in my room."

"What makes you think that Faith? I'm sure no one at Harmony House would disrespect your privacy."

"Well, someone stepped on one of my expensive earbuds and broke it in two."

"Oh. Are you sure it wasn't you?"

"Yes, I'm sure."

"Why don't I come up and see what can be done about this?"

I shouldn't have asked. I should just insist.

Honor disconnected before Faith could tell her not to bother. She nipped up the steps to the porch and walked quickly around to the front door and through. Mavis always locked up last thing at night. Faith must have returned early from the concert. She knocked politely on the door and thought she heard an exasperated sigh from inside. She knocked again. This was no time to back down. With any luck Faith would not have had a chance to tidy up and the true situation would be obvious.

"Who is it?"

"It's your Aunt Honor, of course. May I come in?"

The door opened an inch or two and Faith's face appeared. When she saw the determined look on her aunt's face she opened up enough to let her slip inside.

The room was worse than Mavis had described. Honor had a hard time keeping her mouth closed. Her instinct was to start in on the girl at once but she supressed that long enough to attend to the matter she had most recently been informed about.

"Where's this earbud thing?"

Faith produced it in her outstretched hand. It was small, blue and broken.

"Where did you find it?"

"On the floor by my bed."

"Show me where. There's so much stuff on the floor I can't imagine why you did not break it yourself by accident."

"That's not the only thing that says someone's been here. My diary was on the bed and a page was turned. Someone's been reading my private thoughts and I don't like it!"

"Calm down Faith. I will replace the earbud. The draft from opening the door could have turned one page. Who in this house would want to read your diary?

Look around you, my girl. There's a more important issue here. I can see you need to spend time on cleaning up this mess. Your diary should be in a drawer with the earbuds and your clothes should be hung up in the closet. How long is it since you washed the sheets or the towels? Everyone here is responsible for their own room and the contents, you know.

This was the guest suite before you arrived, Faith. You took ownership on the understanding the room could one day be returned to its original purpose. It would cost me, and you, a great deal of money to replace fixtures, furniture or carpeting and I would be very embarrassed to disappoint the other women here if those replacements became necessary."

Faith had never heard her aunt speak in this tone before. She sounded really upset. Faith looked around the room and into the washroom with new eyes and she could see it was a disaster. She always meant to spend time on a clean-up but days had turned into weeks this summer, and she had put it off one too many times. She had not intended to cause this kind of trouble. She knew how lucky she was to be in this fine home and not in some scuzzy foster place with five other kids around her.

"I apologize, Aunt Honor. I am really sorry for the way this looks. I know it's stupid of me."

There was a sincere sound in Faith's voice and she was looking shamefaced as she cast her eyes around the suite remembering how smart and clean it looked when she first took it over.

Honor was relieved and anxious not to delay one more day so she could report to Mavis and Hilary that all had been restored to its former pristine condition.

"I'll help," she said. "You strip the bed and collect the towels. There's a spare set of linens in the bottom drawer of the dressing table. I'll do the bed and we'll dust the surfaces with a damp face cloth and take all this washing to the elevator and down to the laundry area. No one's around at this time of night. I'll start the first load and you can finish tomorrow."

Faith simply nodded and fetched the clean linen. She grabbed the four smudged pillow cases and began to stuff them with the dirty clothes and towels strewn over the floor. She quickly saw clumps of her blonde hairs tangled beneath the towels and wiped the worst out of the sink and off the floor of the washroom before her aunt could see them. When she went to dispose of the hair, she found the garbage bin was already overflowing with tissues and discarded and broken items of make-up. She turned to the bottom of her closet and dragged out a plastic shopping bag in which to hide the debris. As she worked at top speed she wondered how she had allowed this to happen. The accumulation had been invisible to her for weeks, if not months. Was she trying to destroy the room she was given? Was this some kind of protest or was it the way she always lived before Harmony House?

Certainly she never lived in a room this nice before. Most of the places they rented were dark, dingy basements with old shabby furniture. Often she and her Mom were sharing a room or a bed. They really did not have many clothes to scatter around so it was easy to keep things off the floor. Was the problem that she never before had stuff she could afford to be careless with? That seemed to be a ridiculous reason for this disaster.

As she cleared the space, she cleared her mind. She did not feel this was her very own room in the first place. It was borrowed. Temporary. Like all the other rooms of her childhood it was not permanent.

She suddenly realized she did not know how to take pride in a room. Her mother moved them along before there was a chance to do what Honor called 'housework'. Jolene's family room in the basement of her Westmount home where the group studied was like a palace every time she went there. That was how normal people behaved. They cleaned up after themselves. They cared about their surroundings.

If she, Faith Joan Jeffries, was ever going to have a normal life and escape her childhood traumas, she must take on this duty as part of the normalizing process.

She got down on her hands and knees with one of the wet towels and washed the floor. Then she checked under the bed and found several lost items she had given up on. Her Aunt Honor was bustling around the room like a frantic bee but the results were evident already. She watched while her aunt folded up the colourful rugs and inspected the white carpet underneath. She seemed to be pleased with what she saw but her next move surprised Faith. She picked up one of the rugs and took it to the shower where she carefully shook it out so that all the debris landed on the shower floor. On her way to collect the second rug she noticed Faith's look of amazement.

"No, I don't intend to wash the rugs in there. They will need a through vacuuming tomorrow. It's an old trick of mine from apartment living. You can wash the worst of the dust and dirt down the shower drain if you are in a hurry, but I don't recommend it for regular use."

There was something reassuring in seeing her aunt use a shortcut. Up until now, Faith had seen only the organized businesswoman side of Honor Pace and this new aunt was somehow more approachable. She decided to ask her about the

'Finding Faith's Father' project, as Jolene had labelled it. She held no expectations of help in that sphere but at least she could report to Jo that she had tried.

The secret trip to the basement was accomplished without incident and Honor introduced her niece to the washing machines and their accompanying liquid and powder cleaning products. During Faith's first busy year at school, Mavis had taken on the task of doing the girl's washing. She, and Honor, expected Faith to take over but had never checked to see if that was the case.

I must keep a closer watch on my niece from now on. This has been a warning.

"We'll put the wet towels into hot water and a long wash with a little bleach to prevent mildew. I'll keep an eye on them and pop them into the dryer but I want you to do the remainder of your clothing that needs care. I'll advise you on temperatures etcetera. I guess your Mom did the trips to the laundromat for you."

Faith did not want to admit that their clothes were often worn until they wore out and were replaced in a charity store. Paying for washing anything that could not be rinsed through in a sink and hung to dry overnight, was rare in her experience.

"Get off upstairs now, Faith. We'll say no more about this, but I trust you have learned a lesson. You'll have a clean bed to sleep in and I suggest you tidy it in the morning before you come downstairs to finish the wash."

Honor expected the girl to flee immediately after another Mom-type lecture, but was startled to find she was still standing by the washing machine with a puzzled look on her face.

"Aunt Honor, thanks for doing all this. I will take better care of everything, I promise. Can I ask you an important question?"

"Yes, I suppose so. What is it?"

Honor expected an inquiry about caring for clothing. She was unprepared for what came next.

Faith was about to take a chance but she felt there was a new intimacy between them at this very moment and she wanted to capitalize on it before it evaporated again.

"I won't go into all the background to this question. Here's the skinny. I am thinking of trying to find my father and I need to know any names you can remember from your schooldays with my Mom."

Honor's heart stopped, then began pounding like a drum. She had been dreading this and hoping she would not need to delve again into the distant and unsettling past of her twin's troubled youth.

She walked slowly to her place of comfort, her desk chair, and sat down before her legs gave out from shock. Faith followed and pulled over the spare chair as if they were beginning a long, homework session. This topic, for Honor, would be much more akin to a excavation.

Faith could see the colour drain from her aunt's face making her red hair stand out in stark contrast. This was clearly an unexpected question. Should she take off now and forget the whole thing? It was basically a hopeless quest in any case. No need to trouble her aunt like this.

She was about to push her chair back and leave with a swift apology when she heard a quavering voice and felt a hand reach out to pull her chair back into position at the computer desk.

"Sorry, Faith! That was quite a surprise. I think I told you how difficult those years were. They were the last time I had anything to do with my sister. Since you appeared and filled in the missing years I have felt so bad about having escaped and put your Mom's problems behind me with scarcely a thought."

"What happened to us wasn't *your* fault, Aunt Honor. Mom was a dipstick addict. She never acted like other Moms. She left me alone at night for years in bad places. I am beginning to understand how wrong all that was. She couldn't have loved me at all."

"No, no, Faith! Don't blame her. She did her best under the most difficult circumstances imaginable. She kept you with her instead of abandoning you. She must have worked nights to keep you both alive when you were too small to go to school. She loved you. She saved you although she could not save herself."

Faith's eyebrows shot up. This was a new way of looking at things. Ever since she landed at Harmony House her thinking had been turned upside down over and over again. This was just one more in a long line of mental adjustments reversing her beliefs about all she had known previously.

"Wow! I'll have to think about that. Do you want me to leave now?"

Honor had to stop herself from saying "Go now, please!" It would be an easy escape but this question was not going away that easily.

"I can't promise to remember anything useful for your search, Faith, but it's your right to want to know your father. I'll think back to our schooldays and see what I can uncover. It's a time I put behind me a long time ago. For your sake I will try my best."

Faith was touched by the sincerity in her aunt's voice. She had not calculated how much one simple question could upset a grown adult's equilibrium. Honor Pace was obviously shaken.

Faith rolled forward and picked up her aunt's hands from her lap. She had no idea what to say so she just squeezed the hands tight for a second and ran to the elevator to escape before she became too emotional.

If this was an example of what a search for a name could do to people, she would be glad when her aunt reported that she remembered nothing of use from those far off days. This whole crazy idea could be forgotten. There was already plenty to do in the coming year at school. She would just have to think up a different computer project.

CHAPTER 6

Despite all her protestations to Jolene and the effect on her aunt, Faith could not help being obsessed with the Finding Father project. Jolene phoned or texted several times a day to check on progress and although there was literally nothing to report, the matter grew in proportion to the lack of information.

Even when she was stocking shelves in the store or watching over the older boy while his mother cared for his baby brother at the neighbour's house, a portion of her mind was involved with this new dimension to her life.

What if?

There were many versions of the answer her mind supplied. She tried to screen them out but they swung back relentlessly. First among the diversions was Jolene's vlog idea. For some reason it appealed more than the actual search. The girls in the J.J. gang often spent hours avidly watching teen vlogs, the video version of printed messages. These were focussed on fashion and make-up tips or on relationship problems. No one of their age was presenting a serious real life matter like finding an actual father.

She began to speculate on how this could be done. Her smartphone or tablet could be set up on a stand for a video which could be uploaded to YouTube. *IF* she ever decided to do this it would need to be completely secret. She could not even imagine the embarrassment if Vilma or Mavis or, *God Forbid*, Hilary, walked in on her while she was recording or heard her speaking through the door.

This dire consequence made her wonder if there was a completely private and secret place in the whole of Harmony House where such podcasts might be made. That was a diversion in the realm of fantasy and proved to be light relief requiring nothing more than a scout around the house on the pretext of looking for someone.

She quickly discovered all the rooms other than the winter dining room with the large television, were in constant use. The latter was used more in the coming winter months so, although it was close by, it was not a long-term solution.

Next she thought about the garages and wandered over there to check them out.

The two double garages were reserved for the three cars with the remaining space devoted to the covered cart that was wheeled back and forth to the house with groceries. The single garage was packed to the roof with an assortment of stored items such as Christmas decorations and gardening equipment.

She imagined carving out a little corner at the rear, among the boxes, where she could crouch down with her tablet but that would be uncomfortable, liable to be interrupted, and definitely too cold in the winter.

No problem! Forget it! It was a stupid idea anyway.

She was walking back to the house from the garages when she noticed how tall the one big tree in the side yard had become. It was as tall as the tower. She stood under the tree and looked up. For the first time she noticed there was a peaked and tiled roof on the tower with six distinct sides. Directly under its roof gutters was a circle of small, rectangular, slit windows. She wondered why there would be windows in an inaccessible part of the tower that must be well above the bedroom where Hilary slept.

It was likely a cute, purely decorative touch by the designer for the top of the tower.

But what if it wasn't inaccessible? What if she could find a way into that neat hexagonal room and claim it for her own?

She studied the tree branches with a practiced eye. More than once she and Mom had escaped from rent payment by climbing out of an upper window and down a sturdy tree after throwing their belongings ahead of them. This tree had a spilt trunk fairly low down. She could climb up there and see if the top branches would hold her weight.

No sooner had the thought occurred than she was hopping up the trunk, using her rubber-soled track shoes for grip. The branch that leaned furthest toward the tower became thinner too quickly but a lower offshoot provided a better look at the tower top and its windows. There was a gap of two or three feet between the branch and what looked like a trellis or unfinished frame for a future window, projecting from the side of the tower and leaning on the roof of the covered porch.

Her mind sped through the possible options.

Climb up on the porch roof and use the frame to reach the tower room?

Jump from the tree to the frame and hope it was solid?

Find a way to reach the tower room from inside Hilary's bedroom?

Before she could seriously consider any of these crazy-sounding options she was stopped by the problem of actually getting into the small room. It was entirely possibly that it was a decoration only.

It was never intended to be occupied. The puzzle of why the builder would go to the trouble of placing the small windows in there still niggled at her mind.

What if?

She settled her legs across the branch, held on to a higher branch and studied the top of the tower again. From this perspective she could see the windows and she could clearly see that there was sunlight coming through some of them. They were real windows, not some inserts of coloured glass just for effect.

Suddenly she spotted what looked like a hinge under one of the windows slits. She blinked several times to clear her vision and saw an entire hexagonal section facing her looked like it was intended to be opened up. It was a small opening with no sign of a handle. It was directly above Hilary's windows but once inside there should be enough head room for comfort.

It could be a secret room for secret doings.

A smile spread across her face and her heart beat a rhythm of excitement.

She would try to get up there. She would see if there was, in fact, a room she could use for a vlog or other secret things away from the busy household.

She had no clue how to get there in safety but she would think about it.

She would definitely think about it.

Just then, a figure passed in front of Hilary's windows and she froze in place. The leafy branches would conceal her but she did not move until the figure disappeared from sight.

Yes, there is Hilary Dempster to consider. That observant lady is not easy to bypass. Add that as number one problem in my growing list of items related to the crazy Finding Father project. It's something Jolene will be unable to deny when we decided to drop the whole thing.

She checked around her as far as she could see, then quickly climbed down the tree and brushed off pieces of bark from her shirt as she walked along the path to the front of the house with her head down.

In the middle of the night, Faith woke with a start, remembering that she had seen a ladder leaning against the back wall of the single garage. She turned over and went back to sleep with a smile on her face.

~

After two hours of trying to concentrate on her work, Honor Pace gave up and poured a cup of strong coffee, taking it out to the stone patio and settling into the soft cushions of the largest lounge chair. The crisp air this morning smelled of fall. She pulled her sweater closed and sipped the hot drink.

Mavis waved when she saw her and then returned to her task of clipping back dead or diseased branches. The snip, snip sound made a backdrop to Honor's thoughts.

It was time for Honor to take seriously her niece's request. If she was unsuccessful she would be able to face Faith with an honest answer. The honest answer would come only after an honest attempt, however, and it was time for that exercise.

She closed her eyes and took a deep breath, letting it out slowly until her lungs were empty. The next indrawn breath took her back to the years in Hamilton. The school, the church, the house, the room shared with Felicity where the sisters were able to drop all the outer propriety of their lives and tell each other the truth.

Although they went to the same high school, they were in different streams for classes. Honor worked hard and immersed herself in everything technical she could find, spending hours reading about emerging technologies and absorbing anything related to Google and Silicon Valley.

It was always difficult to keep track of Felicity. They left the house together in the morning and walked to school together but after they entered the building Honor was never sure where her sister went. Often she was absent for all or part of the day, avoiding detection by choosing which classes to miss; mostly the ones where teachers were lax with attendance records.

Felicity would cheerfully admit this to Honor and encourage her to do the same. Honor knew enough about her twin to realize this path was not going to lead to freedom. Freedom from home and its restrictions was an ultimate goal for Honor, not the temporary fix Felicity craved.

During lunch times it was occasionally possible to see Felicity with the crew who sat at the table in the corner farthest from the cafeteria counter and farthest from the teacher on supervision duty.

They were noisy and messy and dressed in weird outfits with rebellious slogans on T shirts, forbidden in school, and worn inside out until lunch when they arrived from the washrooms having quickly reversed them for all the law-abiding students to admire.

Honor tried to remember the names of that crew. The tall basketball player was Brad or Bart or Bernie.

She could probably discount the Mexican kid who left the school after a couple of terms. She remembered the girls, but not one of them finished high school. The chubby boy who always wore the baseball cap backwards had some unusual name………..maybe Morton or Martin? They called him a crazy nickname most of the time.

None of the crew had looks that were any use in identifying who might be Faith's father since she took her appearance from her mother almost exclusively. It was only names she was interested in. What use were these names when the last names were unknown or long forgotten by Honor? What use was this futile exercise?

She took another sip of rapidly-cooling coffee and tried again.

Think! Who else did Felicity talk about?

An unforgettable night in their bedroom jumped into Honor's mind. It was a night that ended badly, and a painful memory, but it *must* have held a clue to her sister's future behaviours.

To reconstruct that night, she had to revisit the bedroom upstairs in the old house. It was small for two growing girls. The twin beds were about eighteen inches apart to leave room for a shared desk against the wall. The double closet was continually in a mess of clothes and shoes and books and backpacks.

The walls were papered with posters of the latest film stars and pop idols. The window that looked into the yard of the houses behind them was always propped open so Felicity could sit on the window sill and puff smoke outside into the locust tree. The room held the lingering tobacco smell and the aroma of sweaty gym shoes and cast-off underwear. Their mother refused to clean the room, saying if they wished to live like pigs she was not going to clean up the filthy pen for them.

Other than for sleeping, Honor preferred to work after school at the library. She hated the mess.

It was the messy room that started the whole argument!

The sisters batted the usual insults back and forth across the room at full volume until their father hammered on the door and told them the neighbours could hear every abusive word. He ordered them to stop at once.

Immediately after the momentary lull that followed, Felicity began to spew out all her hatred and disgust for parents and teachers and society in a low, defiant tone of voice that only Honor could hear. It was an awful tirade against everything Felicity felt was responsible for her boring life.

At first, Honor was relieved she was no longer the focus of all this anger, but soon she heard alarming signs of how far Felicity had drifted from the life her sister thought of as normal.

Felicity was smoking things other than tobacco. During the day she was going to the empty house of a Derek somebody who was not in school. He had promised to introduce her to cronies who also hated school and worked occasionally for friends to get enough cash for alcohol and drugs. Felicity swore she was going to run off with Derek and Russ, who was eighteen and had a van. They would sleep in the van and travel across the country together working when they needed more supplies and doing whatever they wanted with no adults ruling their lives.

Honor remembered the horror she had experienced when she heard this outpouring of venom. She pleaded with her sister to stop and think what this would mean, but Felicity was adamant. Nothing was going to divert her from this golden path. The plan was in place and soon she was leaving everything in Hamilton behind her. Everything and everyone.

Eventually, Felicity ran out of steam and she

collapsed in tears on her bed. Honor lay for hours staring at the ceiling where patterns of frond-like leaves flickered through the moonlight. She was struggling with her conscience, with her fears for her twin, with sympathy for her pain, with anguish that she could do nothing to change the situation. It was too far advanced for her to intervene. This was serious.

After several tortured hours had passed, she did the unforgiveable. She went downstairs to write a note her parents would see first thing in the morning.

The coffee was now cold but it was warm compared to the feeling in Honor's heart. She was chilled through and through. She could never tell her niece about this incident. It would remain locked away where it should have stayed. Faith would have every right to accuse her aunt of orchestrating most of the disaster which caused her mother to die so young. It may or may not be the truth, but Honor was not in a position to argue. She could not defend her actions.

Work was impossible now. Her head was filled with remorseful thoughts and her hands shook from reaction to the effort to remember what she had hidden away for so long.

She stood up slowly. Her muscles had cramped from sitting motionless in one position. She needed to get away from Harmony House. If she should encounter Faith today she could not guarantee to control her emotions. She decided to call a cab and go to town for the day. When she had recovered some sense of normality she would return and deal with Faith's questions.

CHAPTER 7

With only a week to go before school started, Jolene was impatient to get information from Faith.

She maintained a regular text and call schedule until she had broken down her resistance.

"Okay! Quit already! I have a couple of names from my aunt but they're not likely to be of any use. There's only one I recognize and that's the guy who lived with us when I was small and he's definitely *not* my real father. That I know now. He was paid to make it look like he was my dad. He didn't last beyond my fourth birthday before he took off running."

"Faith Joan Jeffries! You really have no clue how this works, do you? One name could be all it takes.

It's all about what we do with the one name. Who is it?"

"Uh, his name was Jar. My Mom called him Jar Jeffries all the time."

"Are you kidding me? That's not a real person's name! It's some kind of nickname and not a cute one."

"Really? I didn't know that. You see? I told you this was a waste of time, Jo."

"Wait a minute. Kids do this nickname thing in high school all the time. Look at you. You are known as J.J. instead of Faith because of your initials. The real point is that this guy is the one who would know the others in your Mom's gang. Give me all the names you got from your aunt. I'll work on the first vlog content and you can approve it."

"What's the point? It's hopeless."

"Do you want to know who your father is, or not, J.J.?"

The question stopped her dead. She ran it around in her brain and checked her feelings. Was this important to her, or not?

The surprising response was strong and visceral. It bypassed her brain and went to her core.

"I guess I do want to know. Let's give it a try, Jolene. But you have to promise to quit when it fails miserably."

"Good! Get started with a journal entry about

why and how and don't forget to include your feelings. That part is for the school project. The vlog is the main thing. If we can get attention on YouTube there's no telling how far this could go.

Hold on for the ride of your life, J.J.!"

In due time the basic text for the proposed first vlog entry arrived for Faith's approval.

(YouTubeTitle:) <u>Finding Faith's Father</u>.

I am fifteen. My birthday is November 30.

I was born in Hamilton, Ontario, Canada.

My mother's name was Felicity.

I want to find my father.

If you can help me, contact this site or this number.

Faith studied these few lines like she had never studied anything in school. She was immediately bombarded with reasons why she could not turn on a screen and announce these details to the online world. She contacted Jolene at once in a fury of denial.

"Jo. This is madness! Even I know I can't just put this information out there for any perverts to see.

I could get the weirdos of the world replying in

droves, not to mention kids from school and what would we do then?"

"Now, J.J. Calm down for a minute. I am not that stupid. This is how we'll do it, so only really helpful people will respond.

First of all, your voice will be heard but your face will not appear. We'll show your hands or your profile in shadow or something unrecognizable like that.

Second, we'll set up a completely new email site and number not connected to your current phone.

Third, we'll make sure nothing in the background is a clue to where you are located.

Fourth, we will not use any of the names your aunt supplied. That's our ace in the hole. If a familiar name contacts you then we can start to ask what they know and check them out thoroughly.

Fifth, we will…."

"All right! You can stop now. I get the picture. Do you have a secret life as a detective or something?"

"No, but I have watched a lot of crime dramas on television. My dad loves them."

Faith still held out the hope all this would be a waste of time but Jolene had clearly gone to a lot of trouble. It required an effort on her part.

"I suppose we'll go ahead then."

"Are you sure? Have you started the journal for school? I am ready to begin whenever you say."

"Don't rush me, Jo. I have an idea for a completely private spot to do this thing but I need to check it out."

"That sounds good. Work on the journal for now. When we meet this week to do our outfits for school, we'll co-ordinate the 3F project as well."

Trust Jo to have an acronym for this!

"Wait! I don't want the others to know about 3F, if you must call it that. This is between us or I don't do it at all."

"Okay, kid! It would be more fun with all the J.J group involved but I see your point. Secret for now, at least!"

"Fine! See you soon. Bye."

She put down her phone and took a deep breath. This thing was becoming real. From now on she could not risk anything being overheard. Her aunt did not know the scope of what was planned and she might never need to know. As far as Honor Pace was concerned her niece had asked a question and received an answer and that was the end of it. Faith would never bring it up again.

Tonight she would find out if the top of the tower could be opened and used. It was Sunday and the smells of the communal meal were already drifting through Harmony House. She would collect a plate for herself and leave with the excuse that she had work to do for school. All the women would be safely in the kitchen at the opposite side of the house from the tower for long enough to let her try to get up there by one means or another.

She dressed in black from head to toe. She dared not wait until dark but with any luck she would blend in with the shaded side of the house where the tree grew.

The first part of the plan was to fetch the ladder from the garage, balance it on the grocery cart and wheel it over to the tree. She managed this easily but the next part would be much more tricky.

She must push the ladder up into the tree as far as possible, making sure it was secure with a length of rope she found, then place it carefully against the tower so she could access the hinged part and see if it had a handle or device to open it up.

She felt it was worth the risk just this once. Chances were, it would not work and she need never try the dangerous move again. She hoped it would fail.

The first part went well.

Pushing the ladder into the tree was easy enough but she had to return to the garage to look for more rope to secure the ladder to the strongest branch.

She tested the knots with her full weight to make sure they held tight.

So far; so good.

She figured she had about an hour before Hilary would be likely to return to her tower room but she did not intend to take that long. One quick try for an opening and she would know what she needed to know.

She eased the ladder out toward the tower, propping it against the trellis-like structure and hoping it was not fragile. The move across from tree to tower took place on her knees, one rung of the ladder at a time. The ladder shifted slightly as she got closer to the tower but it held her weight. At the limit of the ladder she must stand up to test the hinged section of the upper tower while leaning against the hexagonal section and using the guttering to steady her upper body.

She was tight against the tower now and it took a moment before she was confident enough to reach out to look for a means of entry. She knew not to look down.

There were two small double hinges; one above the other, which seemed to suggest this one section was meant to open up but she could see nothing representing a handle. There might be a small notch on the opposite side from the hinges but it was too small for her fingers to grasp.

Just as she was about to start the descent back along the ladder, something slipped and she was thrown against the tower top with both hands out to steady her. All at once, her weight triggered some kind of device and the section with the hinge popped open just enough to see inside. She dared not move until she was sure the ladder was solid against the house. She hoped the rope end of the ladder had slipped slightly in adjusting to her weight and caused the sudden shift. Arriving in Hilary's bedroom through the outer wall was not in her plan but, having made it this far, against all the odds, she was curious to know what, if anything, was inside the top of the tower.

This required a very careful move backward to allow the small door to open fully. She could now see inside. It was a space, just large enough for a small person to sit or stand in the centre. There was some light from the windows. She could see the interior was lined in wood. She calculated the floor was high enough above Hilary's bedroom ceiling to give some noise protection but movement inside would have to be limited. She carefully estimated how far she would need to crouch down to get safely inside the small door and figured it was possible.

The ladder would need to be in a different position, farther to the left so access would be easier.

Her head was making the calculations despite all her fears. This was truly a secret place. No one could ever imagine she was inside Harmony House. It was entirely and totally without any identifying characteristics. It was perfect for her purpose. She cautiously advanced again just far enough to push the door shut with her hand and fingers fully extended.

On the way down, untying the ladder as she went, it occurred to her that she could place the ladder and the rope flat along the basement level beneath the porch. If no one noticed, she could next try the ladder on the porch itself and see if she could accomplish tower access without using the tree at all. Its branches were useful for camouflage, of course, but the base of the ladder might then be visible from Mavis's lower tower windows as well as from Hilary's.

She needed to ensure both Hilary and Mavis were not looking out of their windows when she went to the secret hideout. The climb up the ladder would have to be done late at night when Harmony House and its residents were fast asleep.

She carefully untied the ladder and put it snug against the wall beneath the porch where it was concealed by the overhanging porch floor. As she wheeled the grocery cart back to its garage she felt the excitement of the scheme grow in her mind.

The idea appealed to the part of Faith Joan Jeffries that had grown up with her mother's dangerous ways. Lately, her life had been restricted by her surroundings and the good intentions of the inhabitants of Harmony House. She had learned to conform to their expectations and appreciate their help but she was not yet a caged animal. An exciting adventure in the dark, with unknowable results was just what the old Faith Joan Jeffries needed.

CHAPTER 8

In due course, Hilary reported to Mavis about her conversation with Leonard Harper.

"So he did not believe you are suffering from a degenerative mental condition?"

"Don't laugh, Mavis. It was not at all funny for me. I truly felt disoriented and forgetful. He gave me a test about occasions when I have felt most lost and he seemed to be pleased when I denied ever losing my way home in the car. Apparently that one is significant."

"Well, how do you feel now?"

"Relieved, of course."

"Are you dropping the whole dementia thing?"

"I suppose so, but Dr. Harper suggested I needed to get out of the house more."

Mavis looked up from her sewing in surprise. "Why did he say that?"

"He thinks I am too focussed on this place and all the women for whom I feel responsible."

"He's not wrong there, Hilary. You know you have taken on a lot of work and worry on our behalf. Could it be time to look outside Harmony House? You were always so involved with your teaching career. You are used to being busy but you should not be so worried. I have my garden and my music, Vilma has her dogs, Eve had her painting, and I hope she will return to that soon, Janice and Honor have full-time jobs and Faith has school. You need something to distract you. To give you pleasure without stress."

"Hmmm........ Leonard thinks I should volunteer somewhere."

"Great idea! What did you have in mind?"

"Absolutely nothing! Other than there will be *no* school-related or education choices. I have enough of that with Faith's studying needs. Do you know, that girl has scarcely read *one book* in her entire life? She is miles behind in English Lit. She told me if there wasn't a movie made of the books she was supposed to read, she would fail the course for certain."

"That's tragic! She has the smarts but how can

she catch up on years of missed reading experiences? This will be a challenge for both of you in grade ten."

"Indeed it will! If she is ever to get the scholarships she needs, the path to high marks will be crucial this year. In the meantime, I need to find a volunteer task to give me some slight relief from this problem and everything else."

"Right! I am on the case, Hilary. Leave it to me. I'll get onto my contacts in Social Services and come up with a list from which you can choose whatever appeals to you."

"Excellent! Now show me how to work this Netflix thing. I am going to need serious in-house distractions for my limited spare time, if I mean to survive this school year."

Mavis was still turning over in her mind volunteer opportunities for her friend when she opened the Londoner, the weekly magazine published by the London Free Press, and discovered an entire section devoted to volunteering.

It must be the time of year when community groups are looking for new supporters.

She read avidly, looking for something that would suit Hilary's personality and time limitations. Most of the ads provided detail about their requirements and most were not onerous. There was a surprising number of interesting options but many included some kind of tutoring. She discarded these, as well as the Alzheimer group's request for a talented pianist and the Sari school's need for horse riding assistants for their students with disabilities, both of which had appeal for Mavis, but not likely for Hilary.

She lingered over the job of sorting donations at the Mission Services store, working with people described as 'a fantastic crew' and wondered briefly if Hilary would enjoy acting as a board member for Over 55 London. The latter might be too much akin to Hilary's teaching career as a principal, and she could not see Hilary struggling with heavy bags and boxes of clothing and electronics donations brought from all over the city for the Mission Services store.

It was amazing how much was going on in the field of community support. The article noted that seniors in Canada were known as the 'Give Back Generation'. 78% of Canadian seniors volunteered their time as a helping hand to a worthy cause. Mavis concluded seniors today were of the generation who survived the Second World War and knew what it meant to pitch in together to get the necessary things done that governments were neither willing, nor able, to fully finance.

She re-read the article and finally noticed a small box inset at the bottom of a page asking for Senior Care Drivers providing the 'Gift of Mobility'. This sounded more like the kind of thing Hilary could do. Transporting seniors to hospital or doctor visits or just to the local grocery store would give her a sense of usefulness while underlining how lucky she was to have a car at her disposal. It would also expose her to a variety of different people and to their stories for which she was not personally responsible, and, best of all, get her out of Harmony House for a few hours a week and away from what she saw as the constant demands of the women there.

She carefully prepared a list of volunteer options all the while believing what would be most likely to be selected. It was not possible to advise Hilary further than this. She would choose for herself or not at all.

Mavis presented the list a few days later when they were enjoying a tea break by the fire in the kitchen. The weather was just enough cooler that the indulgence of the gas fire could be excused for a few minutes. Hilary was in a relaxed mood and received the extensive list with exclamations of surprise that there was such a range of choices.

"Well now, this is another indication of how much seniors contribute to the economy. Without these free hours many useful activities would need to stop. I think this is evidence of the remarkable generosity and community spirit of our generation, Mavis."

"Indeed it is! And you can be a part of this effort after you make a choice."

Hilary mused over the list and finally took a pen from her jacket pocket and began to score out the less-appealing options. This was exactly what Mavis had expected. Hilary could never ignore a list. It was her go-to method for getting things done in life.

Mavis sat back in comfort on the couch and watched the ceramic fire logs glow. She remembered her old Ontario cottage and the amount of work it had been to fetch wood and clean out the fire every day.

Instant gas was so much easier. It was one of the advantages of the modern age of which the facilities in this house were a great example. From hi-powered furnace to individually-controllable air conditioning, Harmony House was efficient and easy to maintain. She praised Hilary in her mind for adding the elevator to the house's features. It had made it possible for Honor to get around while her hip was painful and it would be a blessing in the future as she and Hilary, the two oldest of the inhabitants, aged.

She cast her mind over the unexpected benefits of having a range of ages in their house-mates.

Faith brought energy and youthful excitement to their lives along with uncertainties of behaviour, Vilma was a force for such good that Mavis could not imagine the house without her and her dogs. Jannice was the one whose transformation from quiet mousy woman to purposeful, determined, employed worker in social services, was perhaps the most surprising of all. Eve was .... here Mavis's thoughts faltered. Although she had talked to Eve recently she had not yet broken through the barrier the woman had erected around herself. It was clear how she was suffering. She looked worn from lack of sleep and she had returned to the unconscious hair pulling that signified her mind was caught in the trauma of the past. Mavis had seen this kind of regression before. She sat up straight and finished her tea with the decision made that she would tackle Eve in a serious way now Hilary's problem was dealt with.

"Right you are, Mavis! I have eliminated the ones I am not that keen about and what remains are two choices; the craft store that needs volunteers for just two days a month, and the Seniors' Transportation

Service. I'll check out both of these and see what is most appealing.

Thank you for this, Mavis. You have opened my eyes."

Mavis nodded with a satisfied grin on her face. She really did know her old friend very well. It remained to be seen if she would choose the driving option over the craft store. Mavis was confident that was the way it would go.

"Now, Mavis, I believe it's my turn to provide the meal on Sunday. What do you think I should cook? Also, what topic of conversation should be introduced for the good of the group?"

Mavis cornered Eve in her room on the pretext of offering her flowers from the garden.

"It's the last of the gorgeous roses, Eve. I think they will look so good in here, particularly as you have that beautiful painting you did of the rose bush earlier in the summer."

Eve Barton knew well that Mavis was on a mission but she did not have the heart, or the strength, to refuse her entry. There was a heart-tie between them ever since the awful scene with her former husband in the bedroom at Camden Corners. Mavis had saved her life by intervening then. It was something Eve would never be able to thank her for sufficiently. Letting her into her room was a minor concession and, if truth be told, she was tired of her own company and exhausted with trying to sleep night after night.

"My dear, Eve, you look worn down. Is it the old dreams rising up again? How can I help?"

There was a deep sigh in response as Eve gave up trying to prove she was coping.

"Mavis, you help just by being here. There's no one else I care to talk to about my feelings and yes, the nightmares have returned and I am at the end of my tether."

Mavis knew the time was right at last. Eve's barriers were weakened and she could finally respond to help.

"Let's sit here by the window. I always think a view of the garden brings peace to the mind, but then, I would think that, otherwise all my hours out there would be in vain!"

"You have done wonders, Mavis. There's something new to be seen every day. I wish I had such a satisfying creative outlet at my fingertips."

"But of course you do, Eve! Your garden paintings have brought me such pleasure. I know you could do even more if you wanted. You have a real talent."

If was as if she had forgotten about her painting in the dark depth of the depression that had her in its grip. Mavis saw her friend's eyes focus on the garden and then switch to the walls of her room where the best of her paintings were framed and displayed. She was looking at them in wonder. She hardly recalled painting them with such delight, so far removed from joy were her present feelings.

Mavis felt a familiar pain in her heart to see such despair. This was not a new experience. Many times before, in the courthouse, she had counselled clients who were about to walk into a courtroom and lay bare their worst nightmares for public scrutiny. It was so hard to face the deepest fears but she knew it was the only way forward.

Doctors often prescribed powerful drugs to cushion their patients from the worst of the mental pain, but Mavis believed this was merely a delaying tactic and one that could lead to severe addictions in those who were particularly susceptible. She preferred, and practised, talk therapy. It was the only way to excise the mental boil and let the suppurating poisons escape. Talk was the only way safely through the trauma to health again. It had worked for Eve before, and Mavis had confidence it would work again. This present depression was a temporary throwback.

"Eve, my dear, you are now free of Howard. The divorce is final. He was jailed and has been released under serious consequences should he ever approach you again. We have a security system in place. We have two dogs. You are in this room far from the front doors, close to the elevator. You are safe here among friends.

What is troubling you? How can I help?"

"Oh, Mavis! I am struggling on my own. Yes, I am trapped again in that awful bedroom with Howard and you, but there are also the fears and doubts about the years of my marriage that went before the final confrontation. I am haunted by the mistakes I made, the abuse I endured, and the time I lost when I could have been living fully. Why did I allow him to take over my life? Why did I permit him to impose his will on me; to stifle me in every way? He is a brute and a monster but *I chose him*, Mavis! I stayed with him. I allowed the situation to exist for far too long.

What is wrong with me? I thought I was a good person with good instincts and yet I fell into a trap I could not extract myself from. How can I ever trust myself again? How can I paint pretty pictures when I am churning inside with all this dark pain?"

Mavis quailed under the assault to her senses of the long, excruciating confessions that poured out of Eve in an unbroken stream. She knew she had to maintain equilibrium. She must not show how agonizing it was to hear this from her friend; to experience a tiny bit of the trauma occurring just a few yards away from the kitchen where Eve did so much to make life pleasant for her fellow housemates.

What Mavis chose to do and say next, was going to be crucial to Eve's recovery.

She bent forward and wrapped Eve in her arms and stroked her back without saying a word. It gave Eve comfort and provided a few seconds when Mavis could marshal her thoughts and make a plan.

When Eve began to sob, it was the signal that a change was coming. Mavis reached into her pocket and produced a large handkerchief, one of a batch she had saved from her husband's drawer before leaving the cottage. She allowed Eve to weep until she had released her pain. There would be much more talking to be done in the coming days; much more examination of the whys and wherefores, but for now there was a more immediate task to be announced.

Mavis gently untangled her arms and placed the handkerchief into Eve's hands. Then she went into the washroom where she knew Eve stored her large folder of blank paper for preliminary drawings. She found, on a nearby shelf, a box of charcoal pencils and a set of HB drawing pencils which were exactly what she was hoping for.

When she returned to the table and chairs by the window, Eve had mopped up her face and was looking mystified at why Mavis had disappeared so suddenly. She recoiled when she saw the paper and pencils in her hands.

"I can't draw! I just can't do it, Mavis."

"Please give this a try. You can choose paint or pencil. It's up to you which medium you prefer but you must draw this darkness out of your soul in any way, or any form, that helps. Draw any symbol or scene. Draw as if your life depends on it. Draw until the pages are full. Draw until you fall asleep.

Tomorrow we will burn these drawings on a pyre in the garden and you will be done with them.

Then the healing can begin."

Mavis Montgomery spoke with such conviction that Eve could not resist. It was a strange idea but it was something that might work. Nothing else had. She picked up the charcoal and a page of pure white, clean paper and began to scrawl black lines and curves randomly across the paper.

She did not notice when Mavis quietly left the

room to go to the kitchen and prepare a tray of coffee and food. Eventually Eve would exhaust herself and require nourishment. After that she would need sleep above all. It would be her first deep, healing sleep in many weeks, and the first step toward sanity again.

CHAPTER 9

Faith prepared well. She found an old T shirt and cut it in two. She intended to tie the cloth on the ends of the ladder that would be leaning against the tower. On her first attempt to get inside the tower top she would not carry anything. This was to be a trial run to check out safety and the time it took to set up and remove the ladder.

She felt excited and not a little apprehensive as she waited for darkness. She opened her room door and listened until the house was silent, then tiptoed outside, lifted up the ladder and carefully tipped it over the porch railing and onto the tower wall. The top of the ladder, now padded, was placed between two of Hilary and Mavis's windows. Fortunately, the women had drapes which were pulled shut against the evening air.

Faith was wearing jeans and a hooded sweatshirt. Her shoes were rubber soled. She pulled herself up and over the porch railing and tested the bottom of the ladder for stability. In future, she might need a mat of some kind to keep the ladder from slipping but she could not wait for that. Her excitement grew as she realized her objective was so close.

Slow and steady. Take it easy. Listen and watch. Take your time. Press on the small doorway at different spots to see how it opens. Be careful.

She was almost to the point where she was going to give up and try again on another night, when she pushed firmly on the centre of the doorway and it suddenly popped open. Now she could see inside. The space looked good but the most dangerous part of the expedition was still to come. She must leave the security of the ladder and crawl inside the tower.

She listened and waited while she took deep calming breaths. An owl hooted in the woods and she nearly dropped the mini torch she had bought in the dollar store.

Steady now. Almost there. Move slowly.

First she moved her grip from the ladder to the lip of the small doorway. Next she moved up one step at a time to see if her knees were level with the lip. Once she made the transition to the inside of the tower top there was no going back. She realized it was essential not to disturb the position of the ladder if she ever wanted to exit again.

Hands, then knees. Slowly, slowly. Watch my feet don't touch the ladder. Move forward. Shuffle along on my knees.

In at last!

There was a drop of a few inches to the base of the tower top space. She turned on the penlight and scanned the area. The small windows let in starlight but they were better than black darkness which might be claustrophobic. She reached back with one hand to pull the door partially closed. As she had no idea how to open it from the inside, it must remain safely ajar for now.

Her penlight finally reached the floor and she recoiled in horror. The floor was littered with tiny dead corpses of flies, bees and wasps some of which were now clinging to her jeans.

Ugh! Get off me! Get off my hands!

She drew her feet up toward her and pushed the debris far away from her with her shoe soles then she scanned the windows to see if there was a hole that let insects come inside.

Nothing! This must have happened years ago when the house was built. Don't be a baby, Faith!

Once she had calmed down again she assessed the space for a comfortable place to sit while she worked on the vlog content and sent it out to the internet. She could lean against the fixed panel adjacent to the entry one. There was room for her legs to extend to support her tablet. She figured it was dim enough in the light from her tablet that her face would be partly obscured. She meant to hide her hair and wear dark glasses, at least at first. She intended to be a shady lady since all this could be for nothing if she got no useful responses.

On her next trip she would load her backpack with the tablet, a small cushion and a plastic bag with a brush and pan for the dead bodies. Air freshener would be a nice addition. She could buy one of those ones made for cars.

She took a moment to congratulate herself with a mental hug for making it this far. If the return trip could be accomplished with the same degree of silent success, she had something very exciting to tell Jolene. After she slept for a few hours, of course.

There was one more lesson to learn on the return to Harmony House.

After stowing away the ladder and creeping back to the front door on tiptoe, Faith had her hand on the door knob when she heard the sound of the key being turned inside.

Oh no! I could be locked out for the night!

She simultaneously knocked quietly on the door with her right hand and pulled down her hood with her left, pushed up her dark glasses into her hair and unzipped the dark sweatshirt.

Mavis opened up the door and was astonished to see who was there.

"Faith! What on earth are you doing outside? I thought you were fast asleep by now."

"Sorry, Mavis! I was restless because of First Day school nerves and I went for a walk in the cool air to see if it would make me sleepy. I forgot the time."

"Well, you are lucky. I usually lock up before this. You don't want to be stuck out there for a whole night, do you?"

"No, of course not. I'll be careful in future. Thanks, Mavis."

Safely behind her own room door, Faith breathed normally again while absorbing the impact of this new knowledge. *Mavis Montgomery locks the front door just after dark each night which means she stays up later than I thought. I must get a key made for the door. There's a place in the mall that makes keys. And I need to be super careful at, or near, those tower windows in future.*

"You did what?

Where was it? You did this at night and no one heard you, or saw you?

J.J. I am impressed! It sounds like a perfect secret hideaway.

When are you going back there? I have the YouTube site set up for you. You can start right away.

Are you sure it's safe? I remember the tower and it seemed pretty high up.

No, no one can hear me at the moment. I'm inside my bedroom closet with the door shut.

Yes, I'll keep this totally between us. Don't worry! But I must say this is very exciting and a bit spooky. What if you get a response and find your father?

No! No! I understand you can't think that far ahead. No guarantees, of course. It's the internet after all and we will have to be cautious. I'll see you in school tomorrow.

Well done, kid!"

Jolene's response was very satisfying but such conversations would need to be in school time in future. Faith could not risk anyone at home overhearing her. Today was Labour Day and tomorrow was the start of the school term. She would set out her outfit for school and make her preparations for the first online vlog. Then she would take a nap. This was going to be a very busy term. It would be Thanksgiving before she knew it. She wondered if, by then, she might have something special to be thankful for.

No point in dwelling on that thought. One day at a time. One vlog at a time.

On the evening of Labour Day, Faith's first video went out. The basic lines were written on a card Faith held up to the camera. She then added some personal comments about how difficult it is not knowing your real parents and how her mother had secrets she never explained before her early death.

"It's tough to hear about this family stuff later on, when you should have known it all along. I think secrets can be dangerous so I am trying this way to get the truth out in the open."

She finished by holding up the printed sign again, then clicking off. The whole thing took only three minutes at most. It would be posted online in seconds and then Jolene could see if it met her standards.

Faith had enough on her mind related to grade ten's new classes and teachers to worry much about the vlog idea. She had done what she said she would. The rest was up to whatever angel, or devil, watched over the internet.

Jolene, however, was not willing to leave everything to chance. She was up early on the first school day and checking out the vlog site. She thought J.J.'s first attempt was brilliant. The atmosphere was dark and intriguing with the barely-seen face and the blank wall behind her but the spoken part where Faith actually said how she felt had the most impact. She would encourage her to do more of that.

In the meantime, she would send out a link to her Facebook friends, Instagram followers, her Twitter pals, her Reading Group and anyone else she could think of. She might even do a Pinterest board for this while still maintaining the necessary secrecy.

As soon as she finished, she rushed through breakfast and walked to the bus stop to meet J.J. They had arranged to assemble the J.J. Group before school, inside the mall for coffee at Tim Horton's and a face-to-face chatter session, but she needed to have a few private minutes with Faith before the day began.

"Hey, there! Don't you look boss! I love the purple theme you are rocking girl, and where did you find the shoes?"

"Never mind that, Jo! Have you checked the vlog out? I had no time this morning.

Anything happening?"

They were walking away from the school toward the mall across the street. No one could overhear them.

"I don't see a response yet, J.J. but it's too early. We need more content. Give it a few more days and things should get interesting. Can you do it tonight?"

"It's complicated, Jo. I have to be very careful."

"Please try to keep it up for a few more sessions. What you did is amazing! Very spooky and fascinating. Your own spoken stuff was ace. You will get responses for sure!"

"Yeah, but what kind of responses? I am not convinced it's worth my time and effort."

"Think of the long game, J.J. This could be life-changing for you.

Look! There's the gang!"

First Day of Grade Ten.

There was too much going on for Faith Joan Jeffries to think of anything other than classes, teachers and assignments. At least she had a head start on the computer science class. She only hoped her teacher would be supportive of her personal quest. She also worried about the Community work hours she had to fulfill this year. It was going to be a challenge from beginning to end.

It would be best if the 3F project died an early death. She managed this long without her real father.

What difference would it make if she did find him? She had a place at Harmony House which was better than anything she had known before. She even had a real blood relative in Aunt Honor. Along the way, through schools, foster care and elsewhere, she had met many kids who had a lot less security in their lives. Maybe it was time to stop asking for the impossible.

CHAPTER 10

Louise Ridley set up an observation post in the back bedroom upstairs, from where she could watch the comings and goings next door at Harmony House. She placed a table and chair by the window and placed on the table a pair of binoculars and notepaper with a pen. She was considering ordering a recording device for her notes in case they would be useful for a future court case or prosecution.

As far as she was concerned, there were unusual, and possibly illegal, things happening in the busy house.

For example, when the neighbourhood barbecue was arranged by her Dennis, not one of the residents mentioned the girl. Why were they keeping her secret? It was pure luck that she discovered her in the first place. She was following the dog lady's progress into the woods one early morning when she noticed the girl approaching the back of the house and entering through the window wall. She almost called the police then, but shortly after this the pudgy one with the red hair came out and waved at the gardener, Mavis, and she looked fine. Not like a person whose house had just been invaded by some teenager thief.

For months she watched and never saw the girl again until she caught sight of her crossing the side lawn to the garage with the tall bossy one, called Hilary. They went off together early in the day and Hilary soon arrived back alone. This was repeated in reverse, later in the afternoons. After much thinking, it became clear that the girl must be at school. So someone in the house took responsibility for this child. It brought the number of residents to seven. She wondered if this broke some rule of the total number of occupants allowed. She made a note about this and continued her observations.

Naturally she kept everything from Dennis until she had compiled compelling evidence. He never bothered to enter the spare bedroom. He left the house in her care while he was off downtown and on business trips to Toronto. She barely understood his business. Something complicated about insurance or mortgages? Suffice to say it brought in enough money to maintain the house and let her stay home rather than join the ambitious throng of young people who raced into the city each day. The crescent was deserted when the younger couples set off, heading for daycare services with their children. She supposed it took two wages to keep up a home of the size and status of the crescent buildings, but it was too bad it was necessary for them.

If it were not for Harmony House she would be left with only daytime television to watch and that eventually became predictable and boring. She preferred to sit quietly with a nice glass of sherry and her notes, speculating about the busy lives next door.

She wondered what became of the fair-haired lady who sat painting in the garden for several months.

She had disappeared. She seemed to be inside all the time now. Perhaps she was ill. And the cheery youngish one with the dark hair and the Irish accent who had charmed Dennis at the barbecue, where did she go at odd times in the day, sometimes in the dog lady's car?

It was frustrating to be so close and yet unable to find answers.

She tried Andy Patterson on a regular basis all summer when he did her gardening work but he was worse than Dennis. Gossip was not of any interest to him, it seemed. He was quite short with her more than once when she pressed him for details. He was good at turning her questions in another direction as he did when she commented on the recycling bin he built for Mavis.

"So, Mrs. Ridley, are you keen to have a similar bin built for your garden?"

"Perhaps," she answered nervously. "But not right at the moment."

Andy would disappear as an information source for most of the winter once the leaves were down. When he cleared their driveway of snow he never needed to jump off his truck at all, so there was no chance to talk to him. She tried offering cups of coffee. He always refused saying, 'He must get on. He had clients waiting.' It was like a theme with him; always someone else waiting.

But she knew that was not actually the case. She had seen him months ago with dog lady on Wednesdays going off into the woods. They did not stop by the bin where the clean-up was deposited. They went farther in. Who knew what was going on in there? It was disgusting as far as she was concerned. Andy Patterson would barely speak to her and he went wandering off with that woman although he did not seem to do this recently. Likely he got tired of her. She must be older than him in any case. Her smart clothes and slim figure couldn't disguise that from Louise Ridley. Oh, no! She knew better.

Such a pity Dennis paid no attention to her ideas about Harmony House. He could be a big help if he chose to be. Dennis was bold enough to march next door and complain or ask for information. His only response, when she dared ask him a question, was to tell her to take another pill.

Dr. Liston agreed and he increased her medication on a regular basis. No one wanted to listen to her concerns. No one. But one day she would discover something criminal going on in that house. Something incriminating enough that everyone would realize she was doing the right thing by watching and waiting and accumulating evidence.

She had found a new way of getting a better view. When the window of the spare room was opened up wide, she could lean out and crane her neck to the right. Then she was able to see the side of the house right around to the front path leading to the door. The large tree was in the way but when the leaves came down it would be clear if anyone was on the covered porch or walking from there to another part of the house at the back. If she balanced just right, she could see the steps up to the front door. Finding out who was coming and going from there would be a big advantage but only before the winter came and it was impossible to tolerate the freezing air coming in the open window.

It could be that she was missing something in the night hours. She must try to wake herself up and watch from the window once in a while. Dennis would not notice, of course. He took himself off to the guest bedroom long ago with the excuse that her pills made her a restless sleeper and he needed his sleep. She would try cutting back the pills for a few days and see what she might be missing at nighttime.

If that did not produce results she had one more idea to try before the weather turned too cold. She would cross into the garden next door when Mavis was working there and pretend to be interested in her plants and stuff. She could ask about the recycling bin. That would be a good ploy.

Mavis seemed to be a kind person. She had a cat. Cats were nice and gentle, not like noisy, dirty dogs.

Perhaps Mavis could tell her about those mystery women inside the house that were keeping her nerves on edge.

This must be a last resort, of course. It would take huge courage to venture away from her own property and take the risk of being rejected. She knew well how rejection felt and it was much too painful to contemplate. The weather was already cooling. Some leaves were falling from the trees in the forest.

She must act soon before the winter snows closed in and she was isolated once more for long, lonely months on end.

CHAPTER 11

Jannice O'Connor thought her life was improving by leaps and bounds since she entered the community of friends at Harmony House. She was looking at the framed certificate from her supervisor at work. It declared her to be 'a valued member of the Elder Care Team; much appreciated by her clients and a welcome visitor and friend.' It was a lovely thing to have, for sure. It proved all her years of caring for her parents in that old house, stuffed with memories of other lives, was a worthwhile teaching experience. Truly, she had no trouble at all with the courses online or in-house at London's Westervelt College. She did even better with the practical exams. It was all easy-peasy for her. She even helped the younger girls with bed baths and how to help an old person into a wheel chair without damaging their legs. In fact she had enjoyed the whole process.

And now she was seeing the rewards. Her new life was opening up and expanding as every month passed. With the driving licence she could seriously start to save for her own little car. She put aside every month the money she earned by doing the small amount of housecleaning in Harmony House.

It was so good to see the money accumulating. Vilma said she could lease a car rather than buying one outright. She said she would find her a second-hand car company that offered lease-to-buy options.

Really truly! There was no end to the wonders of that woman. She was a source of all the information a person could ever want. Vilma's life had been so totally different from anything Jannice had known. Vilma had two marriages, travelled the world, acquired beautiful homes and clothes and even inherited that wonderful time-share cottage on the beach in Jamaica. Whenever she thought about that incredible week in February she remembered, with such a thrill, the sunlight on the crystal-clear sea, the soft sand under her bare feet, the starlit nights and the company of one gentleman named Mitchell Delaney.

"I cannot wait any longer. The poor man has not

had a reply from me. He'll be thinking I don't care for his interest when *I know* I'm just scared."

Talking aloud was a way she found to help her make decisions.

She turned around and went to her door. She would not waste another minute. One thing she had learned since coming to Harmony House was that fortune favours the bold. She would be bold and ask Vilma's advice.

She tapped on Vilma's door and heard a muffled bark from Astrid who was the more watchful one of the two.

Vilma shushed her dog and opened up the door.

"It's you, Jannice! I'm glad to see you. I want to talk to you about something."

"Now, isn't that amazing! I'm on a similar mission but you start first. Mine can wait a bit."

"Hmm… I think yours should be first. There's a wrinkle on your forehead that tells me you are worried.

Spit it out, my dear. We can't have London's finest personal care worker with matters on her mind distracting her from her important work."

"Oh, Vilma, you are such a tease! It's about that man Mitchell Delaney. He's asked me to go to Quebec City over Christmas to discuss my life story for a possible publication of some kind and I don't think I can do it."

"This is extraordinary, Jannice! I knew you and he had long talks in Jamaica but I did not realize things had moved on this far. He's an author isn't he? You must go. It could be something very special for you."

"I do want to go. He's a proper gentleman and will pay my travel and for a hotel room. The thing is I have another invitation for Christmas and I can't really refuse it."

Vilma had to sit back and consider for a moment how her friend's life had changed. The little mousy person that Jannice once was, had been transformed. Where her life had once circled around that awful, dingy house in a run-down part of London, she was now a woman with choices she could never have imagined back then. Clearing out the old home had cleared out her mind as well and she was a new person.

"You surprise and delight me all the time Jannice O'Connor. Pray tell, who is your other suitor?"

"Oh my! Not at all! Neither of them is a suitor! It's the O'Connor brother and sister who bought the house in Old East London from me who have invited me for Christmas dinner. It's very kind of them and I do want to hear how they are doing. I just can't decide which invite should get priority."

"I can help you with that, Jannice. *Do both!*

Have Christmas dinner with the O'Connors and then go off to Quebec and meet with Mitchell Delaney. You can arrange time off from work during the holidays if you ask early enough. If you fly to Quebec City you will save hours of travelling on the train. You should spend a few days there. It's a beautiful and historic city, well worth exploring."

Vilma sat back and stroked Oscar's head. Problem solved.

But when she looked up again she saw confusion written all over her companion's face.

"What's wrong?"

"Do you mean it's all right to be away from Harmony House for Christmas and also to travel that far to meet a man I don't know all that well?"

"Jannice, my dear, dear woman; you live here but you are not tied to the place every single day. It's time you had adventures on your own. The O'Connors are friends already. Mitchell Delaney is a new friend. You can keep in touch by phone. Quebec City is not Darkest Africa. You will love it there. Most people speak better English than we do. If the life story idea takes off, it could be the start of something very interesting for you. It's time you lived a little!"

For Vilma that seemed to be the end of the matter, but for Jannice a whole new horizon had been opened up and it would take time to catch up with the new vision Vilma had presented.

Me, Jannice O'Connor, on a plane and flying across the country to meet an author and stay in a hotel all by myself? Ma and pa would turn in their graves if they suspected such a thing could happen to their meek and mild little girlie.

She coughed once or twice, trying to clear her brain. The dogs moved closer in case she needed help, then followed after Vilma as she went to pour water into a glass for Jannice.

"Are you all right?"

"Yes, I'm fine! Just a little shocked. Now what did you want to ask *me* about?"

Vilma settled down in her chair again and her expression changed to one of wonder.

"Strangely enough, I've been giving you advice that I should have given to myself. Andy Patterson wants to enter the dogs into a show to see if they are as good as he thinks they are. The show is quite far away in Northern Ontario and we would need to stay there for a day or two. It's an indoor competition for all breeds and I have only a few weeks to make up my mind. Andy has already made entry applications."

"Is it also at Christmas?"

"No. It's in early November."

"I don't see the problem. It sounds like a great thing for the dogs. You have done grand work with them."

Vilma looked down at her dogs and knew Jannice was right. The dogs were ready. Andy had prepared them well.

"It's me who has the problem. I don't particularly like Andy Patterson. He has taken over parts of my life for his own purposes and I am not sure I am comfortable with it."

"But I thought you were getting along splendidly! Haven't you been out to his farm every week all summer? Don't you feel you know him by now?"

"Jannice, he's had a very difficult life. He does not want to be known and I am not interested in a relationship. I appreciate what he's done for my dogs but going off on this trip might give him ideas I am not willing to consider. I promised myself never to get tangled up with another man for the rest of my days. I am independent financially. What more could a troubled man bring to me?"

There was no good answer to this question and Jannice O'Connor was not qualified to provide one.

And yet, Vilma had contributed so much to her. She owed her some kind of response.

She searched her mind for something, *anything,* that might be helpful.

"Well now, Vilma. I can see this is worrying for you. Could you possibly think of it only as an opportunity for the dogs? You would likely be helping this man do something he needs, but you wouldn't be in his company that much. It sounds like a busy time. Perhaps, afterward, it would be a good chance to make a break with him?"

Out of the mouths of babes!

Vilma quickly sensed that Jannice, with little to no experience of men, had steered a path through her complex emotions and found a solution. It was, indeed, time to bring this thing to a close. The competition would be the end of whatever the association with Andy Patterson had become.

When they returned home to Harmony House, she would be free of him.

CHAPTER 12

Faith managed only two vlog sessions in the first week at school. There was so much new stuff to absorb. New teachers and new class groups to get used to. The J.J. gang were together only twice in the week for math, and for home room every day for a very brief period before moving off to other parts of the large, three-storey Saunders building. Faith found herself getting lost often until she figured out the

orientation by heading to an end-of-corridor window and looking outside to see if she was at the Viscount Road end, or the one facing the playing fields.

Last year while she was going about with Jo, Jessica and Jarvis she just followed along and paid no attention to where they were leading her. This year she was with a whole other group but fortunately Ryan was in several classes and he seemed keen to buddy up ever since her fifteenth birthday party.

She was glad of a friendly face.

Jolene had not stopped bugging her about the vlog. If they did not find a private moment together during lunch, she left notes slipped inside Faith's locker, saying 'Keep trying' or 'This will work'. Jo had obeyed the instruction to avoid phone calls but she followed up with texts when Faith was at home.

These had to be ignored while she was in homework sessions with Hilary or Aunt Honor, both of whom seemed to want to fast-track her attempts right from day one of year ten.

Shakespeare was going to be the major hurdle. Naturally, Hilary was a big fan of 'The Bard' and admired every weird word the man had ever written back in the dark ages. This made the situation close to impossible for Faith. She hated the plays, hated the language, hated the history...... generally speaking, she hated all things Shakespeare and she could not disguise the fact.

"But, but.... I have never heard such a thing, Faith Jeffries. Shakespeare is a master. You can trace his works in the majority of films and plays written today. He had the universal themes and characters.

We can recognize his men and women despite the differences of our centuries. Their emotions and desires are ours today."

"Not mine! I am sorry Mrs. Dempster. You will have to find another way to get me through this. I simply cannot read this play stuff. My eyes cross by the end of page one."

Hilary threw up her hands in despair. Faith had to get the marks this year to keep her on course.

The girl was right about one thing. Another way would have to be found. She decided to do some online research with Honor's help and look for alternatives. If the right plays were playing at the Stratford Festival Theatre's stage this year, it could be useful to go there to see them performed, although quite expensive. She would not give up yet. In the meantime she had a few months before first term exams loomed up and there was plenty more to concentrate on if Faith was to be successful in school.

There was an unexpected advantage for Hilary. She was aware that her mind was more at ease when she was busy and involved. Leonard was right about that. Faith occupied evening hours and during the day she was helping out with groceries while Eve was unwell. In addition, the volunteer driver position was shaping up nicely as an occasional daytime distraction.

Strangely enough, the quiet, secret moments up in the top tower room in the dark of night were a kind of relief for Faith from all the tension related to school life.

There were moments when she was just beginning to think this father project might be her salvation.

A real father might take her away from all this stress and look after her. He might not require his lost daughter to be a genius at school. Maybe he had heaps of money to spare and he would set her up in a nice house somewhere far from London.

In her more awake, and sane, moments, she understood this thinking derived from lack of sleep. It was nothing more than total fantasy. Pure escapism.

Life was not like that. Life was a drugged-out mother, social services hounding you, running away from problems and skipping school.

But that was her old life. That life was gone now thanks to Aunt Honor, and Hilary and the J.J. gang at school and a clean comfy bed in her own room and all the food she wanted. Thanks to everyone at

Harmony House she had escaped to a far better present. She owed them all so much.

If Hilary wanted her to study she would do her best. If Jolene wanted her to persevere with this vlog for a few weeks at most, she would try her best.

By the time it was dark enough, and she had placed the ladder, and checked out the windows and listened for noises inside the house, she was already growing weary. The climb up the ladder was the most perilous part and needed full concentration. Getting safely inside the little room brought a sigh of relief. She set up the tablet and picked up the Finding Faith's Father card she left there for safekeeping. Once she was connected to YouTube for a moment or two, she lowered the card and talked to the screen in the half light.

"Hello again. Don't know if there's anyone out there hearing me but I am still looking for my father, wherever he is. My Mom is gone now so I can't ask her for help in this.

You see, it's complicated. Mom was very young. Her parents disapproved of her lifestyle, if you could call it that. Mom was not sure who my father was, or else she didn't want to say.

My grandparents are dead but back then they found a young lad who was also in trouble and they pretty much bribed him into marrying her and staying around for the birth so it would all look legit to the rest of the world. He's not the one I'm looking for but I do know his name, I think. If by some miracle he sees this there's a chance he might know the real dad.

Maybe. Probably not.

You can tell this is all very unlikely. I'll definitely never try to find my father ever again.

If you are out there and want to find a daughter called Faith. I'm waiting."

She clicked off and suddenly realized she had forgotten to wear the dark glasses. Now her face was more recognizable although her dark sweatshirt hood still covered up her light-coloured hair.

Who cares? No one cares! The internet is huge and no one wants to get mixed up with some kid who has such a dysfunctional family story. Goodnight and goodbye!

She climbed carefully back down the ladder and slipped inside the front door. The spare key was kept in the pocket of her sweatshirt if she needed it. Mavis must be up late reading or listening to music.

It was the last clear thought she remembered before dropping her clothes by her bed and falling onto the duvet in a dead sleep, still wearing her underwear.

∼

Jolene checked Faith's YouTube early every morning for responses. It was exciting to see the posts but there were no results despite her outreach to other platforms.

She felt disappointed each time. There was something so sad and lonely about the dark room with no discernible features other than the dim face under the hood.

It was the spoken word part of the post that really got to her. It was like J.J. felt secure talking from her heart to the universe in such an honest way, as you would to a good friend. Except J.J. had never had a good friend until the school group came along.

Personally, Jolene could not imagine what it must be like to be Faith Joan Jeffries. She had grown up in a stable home with a pesky young brother but great parents. She had everything she could possibly need.

She had a kind of security she never had to question. For J.J. it was so different. *So very different.*

This last entry actually made her cry. She had tears in her eyes when she checked into the responses and almost dropped her laptop computer when the screen exploded with comments.

- *Hey Faith girl! You are not alone. I had a deadbeat dad. I don't care to ever see him. You will be happier without him.*
- *This vlog is breaking my heart. Good luck to you Faith. You deserve better.*
- *Let's see your face. You could be an old guy on the make.*
- *Are you in danger or in serious trouble? Call this number for help.*
- *I am looking for a sister about your age. It could be you.*
- *I grew up in Hamilton. Parts of your story sound familiar. Did your mother attend Blackstone High School?*
- *Look Faith! You will be sixteen soon. Have a happy birthday and don't worry about this dad thing. Most folk have a missing part of their lives and they do just fine.*
- *I like your name. Let's see more of you. Much more.*

- *Hi there kid! Have Faith! That's a joke.*
  Miracles do happen you know. Try this site
  I like.

There was plenty more like this and Jolene immediately realized she was in deep. She could not deal with these responses without consulting J.J. She got through breakfast fast and grabbed her backpack and ran for the bus stop. She had to corner J.J. and talk to her before classes.

As she stood back from the bus stop, she thought about what she had read online. How would her friend feel about this torrent of interest? How could they weed out the crazies from actual possible information? What if this was only the beginning of a daily deluge? What had she got J.J. into?

Faith Joan Jeffries stumbled off the bus in a daze. She was falling asleep on the journey these days. Some strange inner clock always wakened her just as the bus turned into Viscount Road but she had to hustle to get it together in time to exit at her stop.

Jolene was standing there. What was going on?

"Look! We need to talk. Can we skip Home Room today? You can tell the office the buses were running late and I'll make up some excuse. We'll head for the mall right away. It's still early. There will be hardly anyone around, except a few mall walkers getting exercise. Will you come?"

"Uh, Jo, if there's coffee to wake me up, I am so in. What's the rush?"

"We can't talk here. Hurry along before someone from school spots us."

Westmount Mall was going through a number of changes. There were closed stores and plenty of places where there was little, to no, foot traffic. Jo and Faith bought coffee and soon found a bench in a far corner where Jo opened up her laptop without saying a word.

Faith took a couple of sips and felt the caffeine roar through her body. Then she looked closely at Jo. Her friend was the prettiest girl in grade ten. Her styled jet-black hair and blue eyes usually attracted a lot of male attention but at this moment no one would think she was a beauty. Her shorter bits of hair were standing on end around her face and her eyes looked as if she had recently been crying.

"Look, Jo, whatever it is you can tell me. I've never seen you so upset even when you got that B+ last year."

"It's not about me. It's about the vlog. You got responses."

"Really? What did people say? Can we look now?

Is there anything we can use? I did not truly expect anyone to pay attention to the stupid posts I did. I thought it was a dud right from the start."

"Stop, J.J.! Just stop!"

"What's wrong?"

Faith's excitement drained out of her when she saw Jolene's reaction. Her friend was squirming around on the seat as if she had been stung by something. She was looking very uncomfortable.

Jolene could not find the words to explain. She opened up her laptop case and clicked into the YouTube site, advancing quickly to the responses. Faith pulled the laptop over to her so it was balanced between them and she could read the screen.

There was silence for a minute while Faith read at top speed.

She took in a deep breath and blurted out. "But this has to be good, Jo! There's some dorks and creeps, of course. That was always a possibility. We can screen those out and see if there's anything useful. What's the problem?"

"Have you checked that cell phone number yet? There could be more of the same on it by now. This is only the beginning. It could take hours to sort out what's good from the bad. I am sorry I got you into this J.J. I know you have a lot on your plate this year. This is a complication you could have done without."

"Come on, Jo! It's not that bad. We don't need to reply unless there's a strong reason to believe what's said might be helpful. I can ask my aunt about the Blackstone school one. Anything else can wait. My next vlog will have warnings about how cruel it is to give false hope. Those dorks will find another victim. It's cool, Jo! Honestly. We can do this."

Faith was trying to reassure her friend and it was an unusual thing for her to do. Jolene was the positive one. She never flagged when something difficult presented itself. Faith felt guilty for the state Jolene was in. She was not unaware of the problems, but when faced with a friend in such a negative condition she had very little choice.

"Listen to me, Jo! No one knows who, or where, we are. We can quit any time we want. It's all good with me. Don't worry so much."

Jolene was surprised at J.J.'s sudden turnaround. She expected her to blow up and blame her for everything which would have been a fair assessment. If she had not gone overboard on Twitter and the other social media, this might not have happened.

Then again, perhaps it was not such a disaster after all. Her natural caution insisted on a watch and wait process from here. If things got out of control she would strongly advise J.J. to shut it all down at once. Neither of them needed this kind of hassle at the beginning of the school year.

She now wished she had never insisted on pursuing the idea in the first place.

Forcing a weak smile, she sipped her coffee and tried to look enthusiastic while J.J. talked about the laptop responses. Another one came popping up as she spoke.

- *I have heard about your story. I might be able to help. My name is Mel Jeffries.*

CHAPTER 13

Mavis and Eve had the bonfire as promised. It happened for several days in a row as Eve poured out her frustration and anger in page after page of black images and shadowy, nightmare scenes.

Mavis deliberately avoided looking too closely. She stuffed the pages into the fire pit and poked them well down with a stick so they disappeared into smoke as soon as possible.

Eve never offered anything about her feelings until the fourth fire burned out.

"I can't believe such a simple act can have this amount of power. I am sleeping better already and during the day I have more control over my memories. But, Mavis, I can now see that I need professional help to move on from this forever. You have been a lifesaver. I can't ask more of you other than to ask if you can recommend someone to take this further. I would prefer a female psychologist or therapist.

Don't answer right away. Give it some thought."

It was exactly what Mavis hoped for. She was too close to the whole Eve situation to be an objective person for long term talk therapy but she knew the best female practitioner in London. If Thelma Wilmington had space in her busy schedule, she would be the one to bring Eve out of the cloud and into the life she deserved. She would contact her right away. Thelma often helped out when Mavis had a client at the courthouse who needed urgent help to face her fears.

She would drive Eve to Thelma's office in town any time she needed for appointments. It was the perfect solution to an issue Mavis now took responsibility for.

From the start of the co-housing project, at Camden Corners, she had taken Eve under her wing and she pushed Hilary to accept her as a house candidate even when she was unsure how, or if, Eve Barton, abused wife, would fit in. The subsequent dire events in Hilary's former home could be laid at the feet of Mavis Montgomery. If Thelma could spare the time, she would be doing a great favour and relieving the mind of Mavis, as well as giving a new lease of life to Eve.

Perfect solution.

~

Andy Patterson had made an application for two events in the November Agility Trials of the Stormont, Dundas and Glengarry Dog Association's annual show.

When he received the online confirmation he had two problems to deal with. His sessions with Astrid and Oscar would require more time to work them up to a higher standard and, first and foremost, he needed to be more forthright with their owner.

Vilma Smith was noncommittal on the whole matter. He thought back over their admittedly sparse conversations, to see where he might have said or done something to discourage her from the idea of taking a weekend to go north to the show.

She acknowledged how well the dogs responded to his instruction.

She continued to drive them back and forth to the farm without expressing any concerns about either the time, or cost, of the trips.

She shared tea or coffee with him while the dogs ran off steam in the enclosure near the stream.

She never asked personal questions related to his former life in the police force.

Was that it? Had she been so turned off by his unexpected confession about the accident with King, and his subsequent physical burns and mental depression, that she really wanted as little as possible to do with him?

He thought she had accepted all of that without question but he could be wrong. It was difficult to know what was inside the head of a sophisticated woman like Vilma Smith. He knew she was way out of his league. It was more than likely he misinterpreted her silence as acceptance rather than the only way she could continue while he worked with her dogs. The subject of his divorce and his isolation at the farm never arose in their limited talk over tea and the snacks she brought.

Suddenly he saw her silence as troubling. Wasn't it more normal for a woman to want to hear about his previous relationship? Women were usually curious about all that stuff. Vilma only ever asked about the dogs. Nothing about him. Nothing. Ever.

His mind ranged back to the one time he thought there was a change in her attitude.

Back in February, when Vilma and the women

from Harmony House were returning from a holiday in Jamaica, he looked after the dogs and drove through a snowstorm to London airport to rescue the group when the airport was snowed in. She seemed genuinely glad to see him then. He felt closer to her than at any time before, or since.

Had he done anything to build on that breakthrough? Or had he ignore the opportunity and let things go back to a neutral state?

Damn! She was likely only happy to know her dogs were safe. I never was any good at interpreting female emotions.

When disappointing thoughts struck him, he did what came naturally and got up from the kitchen table and went out to walk along the stream and wear off his energy. After pounding the grassy verge for a couple of miles in the fresh air, he could think more clearly.

There was not now, or ever would be, a closer relationship with Vilma Smith.

She did not want it, or need it.

Given this revelation, it was an imposition for him to ask her to leave London and drive north for hours to a dog show involving at least one overnight stay in a hotel. He could see that now.

The problem remained of whether he could change her mind and get her cooperation.

Otherwise he would lose the chance to demonstrate just how well he had trained her dogs.

He asked himself to be brutally honest. Was his interest in his own success at the agility show, with its promise of a future business, or was he more interested in unlikely success with Vilma Smith?

The answer to these questions was, possibly, the most important decision he had made since his life changed completely with the death of King.

Darkness was falling. Tomorrow he had a full day of plot digging and leaf raking for his clients. Tonight, he suspected he was not going to get much sleep.

Vilma tossed and turned for an hour.

Oscar was whining. He always knew when his mistress was upset about something. She got out of bed and signalled to Oscar to come out of the big cage and sit with her on the chair by the window. The dog was like a big, hot blanket leaning against her knees. The huge furry tail curled over Vilma's feet and she immediately felt the comfort. She stroked the dog's forehead, scratched behind his ears and looked out of the window.

It was dark in the forest but in Mavis's garden the

tall clumps of late summer's white flowers caught every vestige of light from the stars above, and from the solar lanterns forming a lit path through the raised beds.

Vilma saw the gardens in passing several times a day when out with the dogs but she never stopped to appreciate what a difference it made to Harmony House to have a real gardener on the property creating beauty in every season of the year.

Her thoughts drifted from Mavis to Andy in a natural progression. Sometimes she forgot his gardening job kept him afloat. She had more connection with the dog training aspect of his life. He had devoted endless hours to working with her dogs in that barn way out in the countryside although he earned no money from his efforts. Should she be contributing something financially? Certainly he could use the money. Despite her best attempts to cheer the place up, the old farmhouse building was something only a man could love; a man who was blind to his surroundings. She had not seen the one bedroom at the back of the house but she suspected it was even less comfortable than the kitchen and as for the winter months, she shivered thinking of the freezing air that must enter between the cracks in the siding. She doubted the insulation was anywhere near current standards.

It was a shame he lived like that but she understood some of his reasons after he told her about King and the divorce and losing everything. He still had his pride. Oh, yes, that was still intact. He was like a vault, shut tight against all possible incursions. She had never encountered a man like Andy Patterson before. All her serious relationships involved suave types who dressed very well and knew how to charm a woman with extravagant gifts and delicious meals in exclusive restaurants.

She sighed, thinking of her Nolan who had died too soon. Her breath filmed on the window for a second and she reached out a finger and drew a heart shape.

Nolan and Andy. How much more different could two men be? Nolan was older than her. She preferred older men. Andy was younger.

She pulled her mind back abruptly. What was she doing comparing these two as if there was any reason to put them together like men in whom she had romantic interest? Andy could not ever be in the same category as Nolan. Never. He simply was not her type.

She pulled the soft throw from the back of her chair and wrapped it around her shoulders. She was surprised at where her thoughts had gone for that one moment. She had no personal interest in Andy

Patterson. He was a means to an end. She had no need of a man. Never again would she risk her peace of mind and her financial independence by letting a man into her life. She had made herself a solemn promise about it.

I do not need him.

But does he need you?

An electric shock ran through her. Where had that random thought come from? Was that what Mavis had suggested? She straightened up abruptly and Astrid looked up at her in alarm. Cold clarity raced to her brain and her eyes dilated.

She was being selfish about the whole Andy thing. She should have been contributing money for his work with the dogs. How could she start giving him cash now, after such a long time, without offending his masculine pride?

It occurred to her that the dog show idea could be his way of getting acknowledgement of his ability in this area so he could become a professional dog trainer again. She had been uncertain about the venture and unhappy about spending the amount of time in close proximity to him, but that was her own perspective. It was not what might help him. She owed him this chance to get his life back on track.

She would call tomorrow and tell him she was

willing to go with her dogs on the trip to northern Ontario.

All at once, with the decision made, she felt sleep overcome her. She kneed Oscar aside and kept the shawl over her shoulders as she walked quickly to her bed.

It was settled. It was the right thing to do. She would find a way to fund the whole weekend. It could be their last time together. The financial settlement would set her free of him and all his problems.

Honor was happy to see her niece coming to her office area after school once or twice a week. She was carrying a weighty backpack which spoke of her heavy load of subjects in year ten. Honor had bought a supply of snacks and milkshakes to give Faith some nourishment for the early evening hours and the inevitable homework. The girl was yawning already and it was nowhere near supper time.

"Pull up a chair and tell me how it's going, Faith."

There was some mumbling as a particularly large and fruit-filled muffin was devoured. Honor snatched up a handful of paper napkins and laid them over her niece's lap to catch the crumbs before they scattered onto her keyboard.

"Well, it's going to be a tough year, all right. There's a load of new stuff to learn and the expectations are high from all the teachers, not to mention from Mrs. Hilary Dempster."

"Now, you know you are lucky to have someone like Hilary on your side. She's like an in-house tutor."

"I guess so."

Munching continued for a moment or two. Honor recognized the signs that there was more to discuss.

"It's just that sometimes it feels like school goes on from morning till night without a break. I don't know if I can keep this up for the whole year."

"I agree that it's difficult, Faith. You are under a lot of pressure to succeed. I will do anything I can to help you. You know that. You will need to focus on the future and all the benefits a good education will bring to you. Have you given any thought to what you might want to do eventually?"

"*They keep asking me that at school!* How am I supposed to answer? I am barely keeping my head above water most of the time. This school thing is new to me. Remember? I'm the kid who skipped school as much as possible. The next day and the next week is as far as I can see and that's not always a given. I'm not sure I'm cut out for this kind of effort."

This was alarming. Faith was despairing of completing the year before the first months were over. Hilary must be told about the situation and together they must find a way to relieve the pressure the girl felt.

"Look, Faith! Drink your shake and eat a cookie. I am so glad you feel you can tell me how you are managing. You need to keep it real, as they say. I admire your honesty and your self-knowledge, *and I will help*. Tell me one thing about your school work that is giving you trouble right now."

A grim smile crossed the girl's face and she stopped chewing for a second.

"Just one thing, eh? Just one? Well, I suppose the Shakespeare stuff is a big worry. I think even Hilary is giving up on that one. I don't get any of it. The language is weird. The characters are weirder and I don't relate to any of it. I could fail the English Lit. course because of this."

"Right then! Let's get to grips with Shakespeare. Give me a minute and we'll see what's available."

Honor had a project to do. She turned to her computer and consulted Google for help. In seconds a list of print and electronic books and aids to studying Shakespeare appeared on her screen. She gave these a cursory glance and continued. Faith was beyond the point of more studying to learn about the Bard. She needed a quick solution; something more in tune with her own learning style.

A few more clicks and she had it.

"There we are! We can order High Definition film of actual Stratford Festival Theatre stage productions.

These are top class actors and actresses performing the plays in costume and with all the effects and backdrops to make the message of the plays clear for you. This will bring the words on the page to life. It's what good actors can do with even a very complex text.

Now, which play are you studying this year, Faith?"

Honor's niece almost choked on crumbs she was so surprised by the speed with which her aunt found an answer to her worst problem.

"Are you kidding? That could really help me. It would be like seeing a movie instead of reading long, boring pages of ancient language. It's Romeo and Juliet this year. Can we get the play?"

Faith's attitude had jumped from dark despair to bouncing excitement in seconds and her aunt was delighted.

"There's a catalogue here. I'll order the play and

there's an online introduction video that will be helpful for you."

Faith jumped up scattering crumbs everywhere but it was worth the later clean up when Honor felt her arms around her shoulders.

"Thank you! You have no idea how much this will help me. Thank you, Aunt Honor!"

The hug recipient swallowed a lump of emotion in her throat.

"You are very welcome, Faith. The programs will arrive shortly and I'll transfer them to your tablet.

Is there anything else you need?"

Faith did a quick mental turnaround. She took the chance of getting an answer while her aunt was in a good mood.

"I do have a question about the past. Nothing to do with Shakespeare! When you and my Mom were in school in Hamilton, was it called Blackstone High?"

This was a strange switch. Honor wondered what brought such an unlikely question to the fore. Fortunately, she had the answer at her fingertips.

"No. Our school was called Joseph Brant Secondary."

Before her aunt could ask anything more, Faith grabbed up her backpack and ran up the steps to the porch with a quick "Bye!" sent floating into the air behind her.

Honor Pace was left with mixed feelings; happy that she could provide possible school help for her niece and concern about the school name question.

What's the girl up to now?

Faith skipped along to the front door of Harmony House with a happy song in her heart. She felt invigorated for a change. Shakespeare would be vanquished. *Yeah!*

She would text Jo with a disguised message to tell her Blackstone was out. There was still the last response from that Mel Jeffries to deal with, but that could be postponed for now. More clues might arrive tomorrow. Tonight she would do another vlog and deliver the message about misleading responses and how hurtful they could be. She would soften that with a snippet of information such as telling the odd nickname of the man (not her real father!), who lived with her and her Mom until Faith was about four years old.

As she thought about this entry, she suddenly realized where the idea to tell her school pals she was called J.J. came from. Jar Jeffries was the man she thought for years was her father. Her mother referred to him as *Jar Jeffries* in such a nasty tone of voice, but Faith felt more kindly toward him. In her heart of hearts she had wished for years that he would come back, find them again, and save her mother from the awful downward path she was on.

The J.J. must have been in her memory for all those years and when she had to recreate herself for school in London, the 'dad' name and her own initials, blended together without her realizing it.

This shows how much I do want a real father in spite of anything else I have said about it. And, it shows how much I needed to be a new person to blend in with these new circumstances at Harmony House.

Oh, Mom! You would not believe this if you could see me here. I hope you would feel a little bit proud and glad for me.

CHAPTER 14

Louise Ridley rushed downstairs before Dennis left for work.

"Dennis! Good, you are still here. I must tell you what I saw last night after you went to bed."

Her husband looked up from his newspaper with a concerned frown. Louise was not usually awake this early. He generally could count on a peaceful start to the day with his paper, his coffee, and a bowl of cold cereal.

"Sit down, Louise. Do you want some tea or coffee? Don't get yourself worked up like this. You know it's not good for you."

"I just need to tell you what's happening next door. Oh, I know you don't believe me about those women and their strange habits, but I saw something really odd last night."

He got up and pulled out a seat at the marble-topped island and pressed down on her shoulders until she sat. He could feel her body shaking with nerves and hoped this was not the start of another bad spell when the doctor and the psychiatrist would be required. He decided to listen to her in an attempt to calm her down, even if he was late for the meeting at the office. His secretary would stand in for him.

"So, Louise, tell me about it."

She had expected Dennis to dismiss her worries and jet off to work as he did so often. He surprised her and it took a moment to gather her wits and tell the story. She gulped, breathed out, and began, stuttering a bit at the beginning but gradually sounding more confident as she spoke. For once, she had the captive audience she craved.

"I was upstairs. The window was banging against the frame again so I opened it up then went to close it firmly when I saw a light next door."

"Louise, you know Mavis installed solar lamps in their garden. That's probably all you saw."

"No! No! Dennis. You must listen. The light was up high. At first I thought I was seeing things because it flickered back and forth as the breeze blew the branches of that big maple tree, but when the wind dropped I could see there was a light coming from the tower."

"Louise, the tower has two large bedrooms in it. One of the women in Harmony House may have been up late, or getting a drink or something. There's nothing sinister about a light in the middle of the night."

Try as he might, it was becoming difficult to remain patient. These fantasies of his wife's were getting out of control. He really must talk to Dr. Liston again, soon.

"But, Dennis, this light was far above the tower rooms. It was coming from the very top of the tower itself. Someone must have been inside there. Someone was invading the house and that person could come here next. You must do something about this Dennis. I have a very bad feeling about it.

Something is going on over there, I tell you!"

This was a recurring theme for Louise ever since the house was occupied and the six women moved in.

At first it was mere curiosity on his wife's part and then it became obsessive. She believed she saw a young girl coming and going although he had never seen any sign of that. Now there were lights in a tower that had a very high hexagonal top, no doubt sealed tight against any incursion.

He was becoming afraid of what came next. What if one day when he was at work, Louise marched over to their neighbours and accused them of all kinds of misdemeanours? He felt the women he had met at the barbecue were sensible types but it could result in a harassment suit, or worse, if the behaviour of his wife persisted.

He patted Louise on the back and made soothing noises. Then he went over to the Keurig and selected a green tea pod, bringing it back to a sobbing Louise as soon as the boiling water had poured into her cup.

"There, there, dear! I promise I'll do something to put your mind at rest. Sip this tea and take a pill now. You'll feel better soon."

As he spoke, he was calculating how fast he could get downtown and how soon he could contact Dr. Liston. It could be time for Louise to be committed for her own safety.

~

Andy Patterson was in high good spirits as he approached Harmony House. The crescent was the last stop on his Wednesday route before heading home.

He was making good time today. Mrs. Ridley had

not appeared to bother him with questions for once. He thought he might catch sight of Vilma coming from the forest with the dogs and ask her about the trip to the dog show. He was now prepared to drop the whole matter if she decided to refuse the opportunity. He knew she would never let him take the dogs without her. She thought his truck was not a safe place for transporting dogs and would insist on taking her car with the dog restraints in the back seats.

That is if she chose to go. An unlikely prospect at best.

He had thought long and hard about what he would say to her, face to face. He came to the conclusion that he valued her friendship, such as it was, and he would not risk losing that friendship even if his ambitions to set up a business training dogs was going to falter. Without his conscious cooperation, Vilma Smith and her dogs had become an important part of his life. He looked forward to seeing her and, he suspected, it was not all about the dogs any more.

Be that as it may, he was prepared to back down and not show his disappointment. At the moment he needed a decision and the peace of mind that would bring. If, when she reacted badly, he had to retreat into his cold lonely life again, it was the price he was prepared to pay for this one chance at winning all the marbles.

With one eye watching the forest border, he was finishing raking the maple leaves under the big tree when he caught sight of something out of place. A long ladder was lying tight against the porch below the railing. It had some kind of padding on the top rungs. He wondered if Hilary or Mavis had employed a painter. He felt a little annoyed as he had offered to do any small jobs around the house that they might need. He checked the siding on the side of the tower for marks or blemishes. The house was new but the long branches of the maple might have caused scratches. He made a mental note to mention tree trimming to Mavis and was about to turn away when he noticed a section of the wall at the very top of the tower had detached from the rest and now projected outward by a few centimetres.

That could be a big problem. Rodents, or even a raccoon, would be happy to take up residence in such a nice winter home. A lot of damage would be done over one winter. It would be expensive to repair.

"Hi, Andy! Can you spare a minute to talk?"

It was Vilma calling from the tree line. The dogs were wagging their tails, anxious to greet him.

All thoughts of talking to Mavis evaporated as his

heart beat increased and he walked briskly over to meet Vilma. This was his chance to get an answer.

"I need to ask you......"

"I need to tell you......"

They spoke simultaneously and it was so unlikely an event that the usual tension broke apart and they dissolved in laughter. The dogs joined in with excited yelps. They could sense the excitement of the moment and did not want to be left out of it.

"You go!"

"No, *you* first!"

"All right, but you have to come inside for a bit. I've been out for an hour walking these two and I am desperate for a hot drink. Will you come?"

He nodded agreement and bent to scratch behind the ears of Astrid and Oscar, admiring their bright eyes and splendid coats. They really were the most beautiful specimens. It would break his heart to say good bye to them and the training work he so enjoyed.

They went up to the front door and inside, with Vilma chattering away about the weather. He heard none of the details as he was rehearsing his speech in his mind. He waited while she cleaned off the dogs' feet, then he followed along to the kitchen where she poured two coffees at the kitchen countertop. Finally, he could wait no longer.

"Vilma Smith, will you please come with me to the dog show?"

She immediately recognized that this was the introduction she had waited for. It was also the first time Andy Patterson had actually asked her for anything. Everything he had done with, and for, her dogs, had been given freely. She could not now refuse this one important request.

Many things passed through her mind in a spilt second. She would find a way to pay for the entire trip.

She would try to get to know him. She would be patient. She would be supportive if the dogs performed badly. But what emerged from her mouth was just one word.

"Yes."

~

Hilary Dempster had not slept well so she woke in a bad mood. She had a busy day ahead with a volunteer appointment to take an elderly man to a hospital at noon and a very important session after school with Faith to which she was not looking forward. It was time to lower the boom on this refusal to deal with Shakespeare. The current Stratford program was not going to be helpful. They had included the Romeo and Juliet play in last year's offerings so that idea went out the window. The girl would just have to knuckle down.

She heard voices as she walked along the upper hall toward the kitchen for one of Eve's delicious muffins. It was so nice that such treats were once more appearing ever since Eve started feeling better.

Mavis had a hand in Eve's recovery, for sure, but she was being discreet about the details.

Hilary had missed those muffins all summer although they probably did no favours for her waistline.

That deep masculine voice must be Andy's. He and Vilma were having some kind of heated discussion in the kitchen. Hilary did want to talk to Andy about a couple of things, but she hesitated to interrupt them. It could be something personal. For months she had suspected there was more to this dog training business than Vilma would admit to. Andy was a very fit, good-looking man. Even at her own advanced age she could see the attraction quite clearly. People thought older women had lost their sex drive but they were quite wrong about that. The right man coming along at the right moment could waken them up in no time at all.

Oh, well! She would just go back to her room and make a note to tell Andy she had definitely heard some creature scrabbling about in the roof over her bedroom. He, or someone he could recommend, should go up there and inspect the roof for holes before they were overrun with squirrels or mice or worse. All God's creatures were looking for a warm indoor home for the winter, but Hilary Dempster was not about to provide one in this case.

She stomped back along the hall and promised herself a large fruit explosion muffin from Tim Hortons. She might get one for James Mackenzie to cheer him up after his appointment. He was a nice old fellow in his early eighties. He had a fine Victorian house on Rideout Street that could use some foliage trimming at the front. He dressed well with a suit, a hat and a cane. She noticed his polished shoes. She thought he could well afford to pay for a cab to and from St Joseph's Hospital but she surmised he just wanted the company.

She sympathized. There was nothing more isolating than sitting all alone in a hospital waiting room feeling nervous, with no one to talk to. She would stay with him until he was ready to go home again. She could plan what she would say to Faith tonight while he was with the doctors.

She remembered from their last visit that the magazines on display in the waiting room were atrociously out-of-date. You would think the health services could afford to buy a new magazine once in a while.

It might be a charitable act to purchase a few decent, current, examples and drop one off every time she was required to do a hospital run. It might cost a few dollars. With the large number of hospitals in London, Ontario, and the equally large number of older people living within the city's boundaries, she could be kept busy supplying reading materials. Still, it was a small price to pay for the health and strength to help others. She was learning to appreciate these benefits and worry less about herself.

It was one of the unexpected blessings of volunteer work.

CHAPTER 15

Faith took a break after the latest vlog to catch up on her sleep. The internet did not take a break, however.

"Look, Jo, we can't pull the late bus trick again. We'll be caught for sure, but we must get time to go over these new responses."

"You're right! What about the Library? We could skip lunch and look online in a corner away from view. We have the same lunch time this week. I checked."

"Good idea, but what do we say to the rest of the group to explain our absence?"

Jolene recognized once more what a huge commitment this Father Finding project had become.

She understood the need for secrecy but it was time consuming just to find a safe spot at home or at school. Westmount Mall was often full of kids getting lunch at Tim Hortons and she could not ask J.J. to come to school any earlier. She was showing signs of fatigue already with her early start to get the bus.

Getting together after school was problematic, with sports and other duties, not to mention homework.

For the billionth time she wished she had thought more carefully about it all.

And yet, there were some responses worth pursuing. They had come this far. It was too late to turn back.

Once settled in a corner of the Library by a window and still in sight of the circulation desk where a library-aide kept watch for lunch eaters and other criminals, they opened up their devices. Jolene immediately set a timer on her phone to beep when they needed to run for their next class.

"Oh, the high school name was a miss but it's still a good question to ask if we ever find a good lead."

"That's true. Did you do anything about the Mel Jeffries response?"

"I'm not sure how to go ahead with this one, Jo.

It's definitely promising. We gave no clues about my last name. What do you think I should do?"

"I think you should do a private reply so no nasty person online, with nothing better to do, can see a way to trick you into communicating with them."

"Good! I can do it right now. What should I say?"

"You need more evidence. Ask for a name or a place or something to tie into your story."

Faith bit the end of her pinkie nail, which was already shorter than the others, then she began to type.

> Hi Mel. You said you might know about my search for my father.
>
> You have the last name correct which gives me hope. Please tell me more.
>
> We should keep this private, of course.

"That looks right, J.J. Slow and steady. Nothing too much until you're sure about this person's identity.

Anything more we need to deal with? "

"Nope. After my last vlog message, most of the creepy stuff is gone, thank goodness. I can erase what isn't useful but there are many messages of support. I guess there are lots of kids out there with sympathy for this search."

"Looks like it. Do you think we can sneak a sandwich under the desk and nab a bite?"

"No chance! Hawkeye over there looks suspicious."

They were about to pack up and leave when Faith's tablet beeped to signal a response.

"Don't bother! It's likely an ad or something. If we go right now we can eat before class."

"Look, Jo! You go ahead. Your chemistry lab class is at the other end of the building. I'll call you later. I need to tell you about the great Shakespeare idea my aunt came up with."

"Okay! Laters!"

It was a long shot, but Faith had a feeling about this message being a rapid response to her inquiry.

It would take only seconds to check, then she could leave the Library and dive into the lunch that Eve had prepared for her.

What she found on her YouTube site set her heart racing and made her mouth dry.

Hi Faith Jeffries

I found you by accident. My Dad Mason often told us the story of how my Mom refused to marry him till he sorted out his life and told her everything about any other women he had known. She heard he had a bad rep. The story had a baby girl called Faith and her mother was Felicity. Names you don't forget.

Is it you for sure?

She replied at once. This was almost too good to be true. Mel's story could be real.

The mom was a smart lady by the sound of it.

The only problem was the name of the dad. Mason was not anything like Jar Jeffries.

Thank you Mel (Melanie? Melissa?)

I think you know the man I thought was my dad when I was a little kid.

He was called Jar by my Mom. Can you explain that?

Also, what high school did your dad go to?

More to follow.

The response was immediate. Whoever this Mel was she was possibly in the same time zone and not too busy to be online.

Got to go now. Jar is a nickname for Mason. Look it up.

Faith shouted out loud. "What? You're kidding!"

"Young lady! I don't know what kind of schoolwork you are doing but please remove it from the Library. The class bell rang two minutes ago."

Faith closed her laptop and fled. She could not wait to see Jo and tell her this news. No matter what was going on in English Grammar today, she was stealing a moment to look up Mason Jar.

◇

"Wait! Are you telling me you didn't know about Mason jars?"

"Look, Jo, my life did not include a mother who made jam or pickled cucumbers in her spare time.

I never heard about them before this.

What's more important is the fact me and this Mel were online at the exact same time today.

What does that tell you?"

Faith had broken the rule about phoning from home in order to tell Jolene about her discovery.

She was locked inside her washroom with the tap running. She thought it was worth the risk of being overheard.

"I see what you mean. It's strange all right. She could be in Canada which makes good sense.

Oh, what if she is in school like us?"

"Shoot! Let me do the math. Jar, I mean Mason was the same age as my Mom when they were forced into marriage. He stayed about four years which makes him twenty-two. Then he straightens out his life and meets Mel's mother and has Mel. Say twenty-five or six at the earliest."

She stopped short and gasped.

"Jolene, *this kid is about eight years old!* "

"Hold it down, J.J. My mother or my brother could hear you."

"Sorry. I forgot. It just seems so unlikely."

"Maybe not. Young kids are into everything these days, much earlier than we were. You should see what my brother can do.

Do you still feel you are on the right track J.J.?"

"I suppose so. It all checks out so far. I'll think about it and try again tomorrow night. What I can't understand is why this young girl is interested in finding someone from her father's past. *I mean, we are not even related!*"

"You are shouting again, J.J. Go off and cool down. Check in tomorrow night and we'll see what you get.

And don't forget to bring that memory stick of Romeo and Juliet to school with you. I'll make a copy. It sounds ace.

Laters!"

Jolene was gone and Faith was left standing in her washroom with the tap running and her brain running on top gear.

What had she got herself into now?

How was this Mason discovery going to help her find her real father?

I need to ask more questions and, if possible, I will need to talk to Mel's father. Would he even care?

Why did he tell his young child about me and my Mom in the first place?

What message did that send to a little kid?

Questions rolled around in her head. There was no hope of doing any useful homework this night. She would tell Hilary she had a headache. The way things were going, it wouldn't be a lie.

Vilma was in the hall closet wiping mud off the dogs' paws when she heard the loud voice from the washroom of the guest suite. She recognized Faith's voice and she also recognized sounds of a conspiracy. She knew from experience that teenagers were not to be trusted too far. She had not forgotten Faith's fifteenth birthday fiasco. The girl's good behaviour in the back of the car during Jannice's driving lessons had not wiped out that bad memory.

What mischief was that girl about to bring down on Harmony House now?

CHAPTER 16

O n the next night Faith made the decision not
to climb up to the tower room. It was partly
because she was tired and partly because she wanted
to get more information from Mel and could hardly
wait for darkness. Now that she had a good contact
it was not so necessary to take the risk of going up to
the tower.

Another thought struck her as she was placing a
chair against her bedroom door and locking herself
into the washroom with her tablet. If she was right
about Mel Jeffries being an eight-year-old kid, she
was not going to be allowed out of bed too late.

Settling down on a towel on top of the toilet seat,
she linked into the privacy setting and left this
message.

Look Mel. I have figured out you must be very young.

If I am wrong about this, tell me now.

She stopped to think about how to go on, and was amazed when a response appeared almost immediately.

You got me. I am eight but very mature for my age. Everyone says so.

Even my teachers.

Something else I did not tell you. My name is Melvin. Sorry about that.

I wanted you to think I was a girl. Boys don't spend so much time on social media usually. I didn't want you to think I was weird.

What? It's a boy! Good grief. What next? This is some unusual kid all right.

Melvin. Pleased to meet you. Why are you so interested in a story from your dad's past?

Once again the response was fast and this one scrolled down the screen.

There are three boys in my family. I am the oldest of course. My dad wants a girl.

My Mom works and she says three is enough. My dad talks about how nice girls are when they are small. He says things like 'Faith was such a cute little girl.'

This makes my Mom mad. She says boys are better. I think she is mad because of what my Dad did when he was just a kid himself. She makes him tell me the story of you and Felicity to warn me against all the bad choices that teens can make to screw up their lives.

So, are you OK Faith?

She could scarcely stop her hands from trembling long enough to type a reply to this confession. Suddenly she had a better picture in her mind of the Jar who had been there in her early life and given up only when her mother began to seriously act out. He had gone on to make a good family life with this female who was some kind of amazing one-woman rescue and recovery service. She guessed the Mom of Melvin, and his two brothers, was a bit older and wiser than Jar….Mason.

Melvin Jeffries you are some top class dude. I am

fine now but I have to say your Mom got it right. I have been rescued from a very tough life by some kind and good people.

You should tell your Dad this. I am surprised he remembers me at all.

Do you think he would talk to me? I need to ask him some questions about when he and my Mom were at school. If he says no that's all right. If he says yes, give him the phone number.

We are not really the same family but I am now pretty proud to have shared your name this far in my life. If I never find my real father I will not be too upset.

Faith Joan Jeffries, aged almost sixteen.

Faith closed up the tablet and put her hands on her cheeks to cool them down. This was totally unexpected and astonishing. She had no idea what, if anything, would happen now, but a gap in her life was filled. Chances were good Melvin's fierce and protective mother would put a stop to the whole online thing. She could not blame her if she did.

In a way it had served its purpose. How Melvin found her post on YouTube was a mystery, but perhaps Jolene was right about younger kids today having better skills and more curiosity than their older brothers and sisters. Maybe it was just her spooky disguise that attracted him.

A sense of peace filled her heart. She had not been forgotten by Mason Jeffries, the off-track youngster who was bribed into giving his name to a young mother and her daughter. His decision to abandon them, four or so years later, was not the evil act portrayed so often by Felicity, who blamed Jar for the very habits and choices that drove him away. Mason was saving his own life and he still felt guilty about doing it.

It was enough. She now knew enough. The Finding Father project had succeeded. Not exactly as she had hoped but in some ways it was a better outcome.

She fell into bed and slept as she had not been able to since the project started. Her final thoughts were about what a fabulous story she had to tell Jolene tomorrow and what a great computer project this would make for the journal entry in class.

Two weeks went by; two weeks during which a number of things came to a head.

Faith stopped adding to the online material and concentrated on her school work. Shakespeare, as performed by expert actors, became marginally more comprehensible. She planned repeat viewings.

Honor was relieved that Faith was more focussed.

Dennis Ridley phoned Hilary from his office downtown and advised her that Louise was ill and under a doctor's orders but she might possibly wander off and be found on the grounds of Harmony House.

He politely asked to be informed immediately if such an event occurred.

Hilary agreed at once and expressed her sympathy for Louise's condition.

"What makes you think your wife might head over here, Dennis?"

He was reluctant to provide further information but in case of some disturbance caused next door he chose to take Hilary Dempster into his confidence as a preventative against the police being called.

"I am sorry to have to tell you, Louise has been unwell for some time now. She imagines things. For example, she told me she has seen lights in your house far into the night in a suspicious place where no one could go."

"Oh my! What a worry for you Dennis. If you

need someone to check on Louise during the day, Mavis or myself would be glad to help out."

He felt quite overcome by this suggestion. His voice betrayed his emotion and Hilary detected a catch in his voice when he responded.

"That is extremely kind of you, Hilary. I may be required to ask you to do this sometime. It's difficult when I am at work all day."

"Of course! Please call on us if you need us."

"Thank you."

Andy Patterson remembered the misplaced ladder and checked to see if it was gone on his next Wednesday visit. When he saw it was still in position he asked Vilma if work was being done on the house.

"Nothing I know about, Andy. I'll ask Hilary. She's out right now. Remind me to tell you when I see you on Friday."

Later in the day, Vilma found Hilary in the kitchen and repeated what Andy had said.

"No. There's nothing scheduled. Why would a ladder be left near the house? Let's go outside and find it, right now."

Hilary was thinking this could have something to do with Louise Ridley next door. Her husband had indicated strange behaviour was possible.

Vilma followed along to be company for Hilary and so she could report accurately to Andy. She had no other interest in the ladder issue. She had plenty on her mind already. Perhaps this private moment would be a chance to fill Hilary in on the Dog Show weekend and get her opinion.

It was obvious, once they began to search, that the ladder in question was deliberately placed tight against the base of the porch and hidden by the large maple tree.

"This is no accident," announced Hilary. "Someone wanted to conceal what they were doing. Don't touch it Vilma. I'll keep an eye on this area now and see what I can find out."

Hilary was considering whether or not she should mention this to Dennis.

Vilma was suddenly brought up short by recognizing the padding on the ends of the ladder. The worn cloth was an unusual colour, tied in place on the top rungs by elastic bands. Faith Jeffries had once worn a T shirt in that violent shade of pink.

She did not mention this discovery to Hilary but she determined to keep watch whenever she was passing with the dogs. If Faith was up to something, Vilma Smith would be sure to catch her out.

The girl was definitely a stranger in their midst. It

would not surprise her if she turned out to be doing something illegal. The girl's family background was dubious at best. It was quite likely Honor, with no previous experience of teenagers, had been hoodwinked into thinking the girl had reformed.

As far as Vilma Smith was concerned, a leopard never changes its spots.

Faith had forgotten the burner phone with the number she had given out on the card information.

It took her several minutes to track down the buzzing she could hear. At first she thought her ears were buzzing from the headphones she used to watch the Shakespeare videos. She shook her head about and tried a cotton swab but nothing helped until she passed her bedside table drawer and noticed the sound got louder.

"Flip! It's the phone!"

Thinking it could be Jo with an urgent message she rushed to answer, wondering how often the phone had been ringing and she had not noticed. Jo would be mad with her.

"Hi! I've got it now! Sorry, if you had to wait. I forgot all about this phone."

There was a silence on the line and she realized it

was not Jolene calling. Jo would have laid into her at once for wasting her time.

"Who's there?"

Visions of pedophiles and child kidnappers raced through her mind from lectures and warnings she had received in school. Her hand shook as she made to disconnect. She would throw this thing in the garbage right away.

"Faith, is that you? It's Mason Jeffries here."

While she was still struck dumb with sheer shock, the male voice continued.

"Melvin told me everything and showed me your vlog. He's quite a character, isn't he? God knows what he'll be like in a few years. He's a handful for his Mom and me already. Too smart for his own good.

Can you talk? Is this a bad time? Sorry for rambling on."

"No. It's okay. I didn't expect to hear from you. I forgot about the phone completely."

"That's all right. It's taken me a while to catch up with everything but I am so happy to know you are with good people. I have had nightmares about you and your Mom. She took you away and I couldn't trace you two. I did try, Faith. Believe me. I know I shouldn't have left you the way I did."

Her first thought was to tell him about the real

nightmares of her childhood, but she thought those stories might make him stop talking to her altogether. She had questions that still needed answers.

"I finally found my Aunt Honor, Felicity's twin. I live in a grand house in London, Ontario, now, and I am working hard in school. "

"That's wonderful news, Faith!"

He really sounded happy for her. She decided it was best to leave the past in the past; except for one important detail.

"Mason, you must know from Melvin that I am trying to find my real father. Can you remember from school days who might be the one who made my mother pregnant? I have a few first names from my aunt but she has no idea who it was. Did my mother ever talk to you about it?"

"Mel told me, Faith, and I have tried to think of anything I heard said back then, but the truth is I don't know. I was a mess myself in those days with enough problems of my own to worry much about anyone else around me.

I believe now, if your Mom knew who it was, she would have told your parents. Yes, she went around with several guys who were a bad influence. Frankly, it could have been any one of them. I am sorry to say this Faith and I don't want to hurt you any more than I already have. I just can't tell you what you want to know. Nobody can."

It was a hard fact to swallow, but not entirely unexpected.

In those few seconds, Faith felt a change inside her. She began to grow up. She was on her own. She realistically held no great hopes of the 'real' dad making a difference in her life.

She was where she was. She was who she was. She was Faith Jeffries, for good or ill.

"Thank you for being honest, Mason. I am happy with your last name. You sound like a great dad for your kids. And, please tell Melvin I owe him a lot."

"Don't go yet! We live in Kingston now. I want you to know you are welcome here any time. I think of you as the daughter I have always wanted. Write down our phone number. Mel wants to meet you and I would love to see you again. Pauline agrees with me about this. She knows I never forgot about you.

Please, let this be your sixteenth birthday present from us."

Again with the unexpected! This man was not who my Mom described. Or maybe he has grown up since then.

"I promise to keep your number but this phone is done now. Goodbye and thanks again, Jar."

Darn it! I called him by the old name. Never mind. It's

*done now. People say things like 'come to see us' and don't
expect it to happen in this lifetime.*

Bye Melvin, you smart kid.

Bye, real dad whoever, or wherever, you may be.

Bye vlog.

*Bye, tower room...........Oops! One more climb up there
to remove all the evidence, then the ladder goes away and
it's truly all over.*

Faith copied the phone number then put the burner
in her backpack to show Jolene. They could dispose
of it at school for safety. Awkward questions could
be asked if the phone was found in Harmony House.

She checked on the time. It was still early in the
evening. She needed to get a few things off her chest
and it was probably good to bring her aunt into the
picture.

Honor had just finished for the day. She went
through her stretching routine before donning her
coat and going out for a walk to use her leg muscles.
The big window wall had been closed tight for hours
so she climbed the steps to the porch from where
she could walk down the slope to the garden.

She almost bumped into Faith at the door.

"Hello there! I was just thinking about you. How's the Shakespeare going? I am off for a walk. Do you want to come along?"

"Sure!" The less said about the Finding Father thing inside the house, the better. If her aunt was going to freak out, it was best to get it done with, where no one could overhear.

They set off along the side path to the garages. Faith followed her aunt who seemed to have a regular exercise circuit and was walking quite quickly.

There was no easy way to get into the topic so Faith just blurted it all out in a steady stream with hardly a breath to break it up.

Honor came to a complete halt and turned around to make sure she was seeing and hearing properly.

"You mean you did this online, in the house, without anyone knowing?"

Faith nodded.

"You know you took a big risk? Any pervert could have snagged you."

Faith nodded.

"You found Jar Jeffries, I mean Mason Jeffries, and he has a family with three boys living in Kingston?"

Faith nodded.

"I should be furious with you for taking these risks but it all seems to have worked out well. Don't ever do anything that crazy like that again Faith Joan Jeffries. Your grandmother, Joan, would have taken a strip off your hide for that behaviour, believe you me! You are so fortunate Hilary Dempster did not find out what was going on under her roof. She might well throw you out for this kind of deception.

Let's agree to say nothing more about it. You had a lucky escape young lady!"

Faith nodded.

"I know it was stupid, Aunt Honor. I'll be more careful in future and I'll take you into my confidence before I go off on another crazy scheme."

They walked on toward the edge of the forest without knowing that Louise Ridley was standing by the open window of her upper bedroom listening to every word and swearing she would make Dennis believe her this time. That strange girl next door had just confessed to doing forbidden things that upset her Aunt Honor. It was something secret with family involved. It was wrong and the tall one, Hilary, did not know about it at all. She must tell Dennis right away.

CHAPTER 17

Andy followed Vilma home in his truck on Friday evening. He was reassured that Hilary had not employed a workman but, in their earlier phone conversation, he mentioned noticing a portion of the tower top had pulled away. Hilary agreed this should be fixed as soon as possible and he thought he could do it before darkness fell, if he cut short the practise session. The training was going very well and now that Vilma was on side with the Dog Show plan he felt much more relaxed about it all.

Vilma and the dogs went indoors and he walked round to the tower. He remembered about the ladder as soon as he went to examine the tower using a strong flashlight he took from his truck's tool box.

He calculated there was nothing wrong with the ladder's location since no one had moved it back to the garage, so he lifted the ladder into place against the side of the house and, hefting a couple of tools into the deep pockets of his coveralls, he climbed up for a closer look.

There was no paint damage he could see from the tree branches, although he presumed the pressure from a branch during a strong wind had caused the open section to release.

It was a surprise to find there was an actual door in the hexagonal top. It was small but still capable of allowing rodents to access the building by gnawing their way through the walls. He oiled the hinges and checked the simple push locking system. Then he looked inside to make sure no creature had taken up residence.

It was then he found a placard of some kind and a small flashlight and a cushion.

Someone had been inside the tower room and it was neither a squirrel nor a raccoon.

He threw down the cushion and pocketed the flashlight. The placard just fit inside the bib part of his coveralls. If he climbed back down carefully he could then examine it for clues.

It was almost dark by the time he closed up the tower room securely and made his way slowly to the ground again.

Hilary, who was reading in her room, heard the noise of the ladder against the tower walls and watched to make sure Andy was safe. It was really too dark for such activities.

She saw the cushion come flying past and her curiosity was aroused.

By the time Andy had replaced the ladder in the garage, she was waiting for him at the front door.

"What's going on?"

"You tell me Mrs. Dempster. There are definitely signs someone has been up in the top of the tower."

He pulled out the cardboard and turned it so the light shone on the letters.

Hilary read the message and there was no doubt who the culprit was. She felt relieved for one moment that it was not an unknown intruder but her anger resumed almost immediately. What was that girl thinking?

Her first instinct was to turn and hammer on the door to Faith's room. A second later she realized Honor must be the one to take responsibility for her niece.

"Andy, I'll take care of this. Thank you for fixing the door. If you will please return the ladder to the garage, you can get off home. I'll bring Vilma up to date about all this."

"Fine with me! You know where I am if you need anything done."

"I do and it's a great comfort to have you standing by, Andy.

Goodnight."

Hilary did not wait any longer. She went along the porch and knocked on the side door, only to find Honor standing on the other side wearing a coat and obviously ready to exit.

"Hilary, I was coming to find you."

One look at Hilary's face and Honor knew why she was on her doorstep.

"Look, it's best if you come inside. I have things to explain."

She turned carefully on the small platform and led the way down to her domain, pulling out the spare chair and taking her usual position by her desk. She steeled herself for trouble knowing this was not the first time she had to defend her niece to Hilary Dempster. The birthday fiasco was fresh in her mind but on this occasion she had the entire story already and she was prepared to fight on Faith's behalf.

"Hilary, Faith came to me and told me everything she had done. She understands how dangerous and foolish her actions were, but I must remind you of her age and of how different her life was before she came under your roof. I think you will agree that she has come a very long way under your tutelage. It's perhaps not surprising that she falters now and again, considering how she was treated before and after her mother died.

Basically she was searching for answers about her origins. Who among us has not tried to do that?

Most of us grow up knowing who we are and that knowledge gives us the confidence to face the world. Try to picture the great gap in your own life if you were one of those who missed growing up in the bosom of family.

Oh, I know a bit about this myself but I am one of the survivors. I escaped in time. Faith was not so lucky.

Please give her another chance to prove to you how she has learned. She has given me her solemn promise to come to me in the future before she does anything in the least little bit dangerous. I believe her.

Do you believe *me*, Hilary?"

The ball was truly in Hilary's court. Despite herself she was impressed by Honor's spirited defence of her niece. Considering she had very little experience in being a good aunt, she was certainly exhibiting the ability to learn fast.

Recent events in her life had taught Hilary Dempster that she need no longer take on all the responsibility for the inhabitants of Harmony House. Here was the perfect example of an occasion to back down and let someone else deal with a situation. After all, Honor Pace was the only known family member of Faith Jeffries. It was her business to straighten the girl out.

To Honor's amazement, Hilary pursed her lips and stood silently for a moment before speaking in a gentle tone of voice.

"I trust you, Honor. You are a valuable part of the team here and you have taken on this teenager with a courage that must be admired. It will not be an easy task but together we can continue to guide her, as we have all done in our different ways. She's a smart girl who just needs direction.

I'll bid you goodnight and leave this matter in your capable hands."

Honor was both relieved and astounded. Hilary Dempster had actually complimented her. More than once!

She raised her chin in pride and satisfaction. This aunt business was difficult, but not entirely impossible.

Her thoughts turned to a small bottle of coffee liqueur she was keeping for a special occasion. A liberal splash of that in her coffee would feel like a minor celebration for a job well done. She considered it was a small treat, well deserved.

～

Faith woke and stretched and felt quite different. Lighter somehow. It took a second or two until she realized the whole Finding Faith's Father thing was done and over. She had confessed to her aunt and made promises she had every intention of keeping.

It was a fine bright Saturday morning. She took a few minutes to clean up her room and hang up towels, feeling as if she had more energy to spend now. She would contact Jolene and tell her everything. They would dispose of the burner phone.

Faith was free today and she knew what she was going to do with the time. Her computer studies class journal would be brought up to date and she would write about her experiences before coming to London to provide background for the project. She would also make it clear she had done dangerous things in pursuit of her objective. Mr. Blakely would appreciate that aspect as a warning to others. For the first time she was not ashamed of letting the other kids in her class know about her past. Teachers always said it was what you did in the present and the future that counted the most.

Faith Joan Jeffries was claiming that future for herself.

~

Louise Ridley was standing outside her husband's bedroom door waiting anxiously to hear sounds of movement. She had not slept all night after hearing the story told by the girl, Faith, to her aunt, the red-haired one.

She must tell Dennis first thing. It was proof she was not mad. The girl was the one up in the top tower doing something. She had a light on there. Louise Ridley was not making things up or imagining things.

There were odd and possibly dangerous acts going on next door and something had to be done about it before the house burned down and the fire spread to their house. Dennis would know what to do if she could only persuade him to stop and listen.

She did not take the pills she was supposed to take before bed and she was glad. Her mind felt sharper.

She was ready to convince him this time and he would know she was right all along.

Dennis Ridley showered and dressed and hummed a little tune as he collected his keys and wallet from the top of the tall dresser. Louise would be fast asleep. The pills kept her comatose till well into the morning and he could escape without any drama. An important business deal was to be signed, sealed and delivered today. It meant a good salary boost. He could finally consider selling this place on the crescent and moving back to town, closer to the hospitals. He knew Louise would soon need professional help beyond what Dr. Liston could provide. It was not beyond the bounds of possibility that Louise would be sectioned one day.

His mind jumped away from this thought but it was becoming inevitable and would need to be faced.

He fastened his suit jacket and took one last look in the mirror, smoothing down his hair and smiling at the image of a smart and capable man of the world.

As soon as he opened up the door everything changed.

His wife stood there looking like a ghost with

pale face and dark shadows beneath her staring eyes. He flinched and stepped back but she advanced and caught his lapels in both hands, thrusting her face into his so he could smell her foetid breath, and talking fast like a demented person about the house next door again.

He was taken aback by this extraordinary physical assault and his brain took seconds to adjust. He heard what she said and discounted it immediately as more raving from a deeply disordered mind.

This could not be tolerated any longer. He could not be expected to function with this situation in his home.

He took several breaths as shallowly as possible to escape the noxious smell from his wife's mouth and slowly unlocked her fingers from his suit jacket all the while making soothing sounds and repeating his assurances that everything would be handled, she was correct of course, it was not her fault, he would take care of it.

Hearing these words, Louise seemed to collapse as if all the air had gone out of her. He laid her down on the bed and she simply closed her eyes and became calm.

He had only a few minutes to act and he did so at once. He closed the bedroom door softly and went downstairs to the kitchen where he called Dr. Liston and reported the incident with the strongest recommendation that the situation was now untenable and Louise must be taken somewhere for her own safety.

The doctor was not surprised. This scenario had been discussed between them on several occasions. He put into motion the agreed-upon plan and contacted the Psychiatric Department of the hospital, alerting them to send an ambulance immediately. He presumed that Dennis Ridley would be present when the ambulance arrived, but in this he was mistaken.

Dennis was facing a difficult choice. He dared not leave his wife unsupervised. Anything could happen when she woke. She was completely out of control.

He should stay.

He must go. The business deal that affected the finances of his entire staff could not be put in jeopardy by this home situation. He floundered around in his mind for an escape. Then, he remembered his conversation with Hilary Dempster next door. He had forewarned her about Louise. She would understand this emergency. She was a sensible woman. She must help.

CHAPTER 18

Hilary woke to a fine and free Saturday. She was not scheduled for anything in particular. She might have a leisurely breakfast with Mavis and Eve and catch up with events at Harmony House. She would decide how much of the tower escapade to share with them, but whatever she said, it would be a touch of drama to add savour to the eggs and bacon.

She was combing her hair when the call came.

Darn! Hope this isn't a volunteer assignment. I want a day to myself.

That hope dissipated as soon as she caught the gist of Dennis Ridley's impassioned appeal.

At once, her headmistress persona took over.

This was an emergency. She coped very well in such situations. It was one of her most valuable skills.

"I'll be right over, Dennis. Don't worry."

There was no time to inform anyone about what was happening. She left the house and walked quickly to the garages and through the gap in the high hedge of trees.

Dennis was waiting by the front door.

"I am so glad you are here, Hilary. The ambulance will arrive soon. Just listen for Louise. She's in the bedroom upstairs. Thank you so much."

With that he was gone. Leaving her in sole charge.

Hilary stepped into the silent house and suddenly the reality of the situation struck her with full force. She had never before dealt with a person who was mentally disturbed to the degree described by Dennis Ridley.

Mavis was the better person for this job but Louise's husband had asked for speed and discretion. She could always call Mavis if things got out of control. The ambulance was due to arrive, he said.

Her thoughts turned to Louise Ridley. What had that poor woman being going through, unknown to all the women right next door? How had she got into this dire state? Leaving her home in an ambulance was a desperate conclusion to whatever had set this off. She hoped there was no blood to be dealt with.

Severely disturbed persons often tried suicide to escape their inner pain.

Surely not that?

It occurred to her to find out which bedroom Louise was in. The emergency personnel would need to know and not be required to tramp around the whole of the large second floor of the house, no doubt alarming poor Louise even more than she was already.

She tiptoed up the carpeted staircase, noting peripherally the calm beige colouring and making a mental note to do something at last about the nasty violet colour of the Harmony House stairs.

No sign of blood. In fact everything seemed in perfect order. She breathed a sigh of relief.

She crept along, listening at each door for sounds.

Nothing, until she reached the double doors that indicated a master bedroom suite. This was the logical choice for his wife's location, so she turned to leave.

Dennis said Louise was sleeping soundly. What, then, was the meaning of the pitiful weeping she could now hear coming from the master bedroom? In all her years she had never before heard such a heart-rending sound. It signified a release of deep sorrow and despair. It was a sound Hilary Dempster simply could not ignore.

Fearing to discover the nightmare scene of imminent suicide, she decided to take action to assure herself of Louise Ridley's safety. In the back of her mind was the episode in Camden Corners when Mavis's timely intervention had undoubtedly saved Eve's life.

She quietly opened the double doors just far enough to see the bed. Louise was sitting on the side of a large double bed with her back turned to Hilary. She meant to withdraw at once, but as soon as she began to understand the words between the sobs, she stopped, frozen in place and listened intently.

"Dennis believes me. He knows I was right. He will love me again like he used to. He is coming back soon. We can go together next door and tell all the women about the danger they are in. They will be happy to hear how I have watched over them. They will be my friends now .... The tall one, the red-haired one, the gentle one in the garden and even the one with the dogs. All of them will like me now. Perhaps we can have tea together in the garden. That would be so nice. Or we can sit on the porch and talk about how I saw the lights up in the tower. I kept on watching out when Dennis thought I was crazy. I know he did but I am not crazy. All the pills he told me to

take have changed how I think. I'll throw them all away now. It's all true. Everything I have been telling him is true. I heard the women talking right beneath my window. There was an intruder up there."

By this point, Hilary was awash in mixed emotions. She was incensed that this poor woman had been labelled as insane. Louise's desperate tears were coming from pure relief at her story being believed. Hilary was furious with Dennis for denying his wife's account without checking on the facts. She was also furious with Faith for exacerbating whatever fears this lonely woman had imagined.

She had to prevent this awful injustice. If she did nothing, Louise Ridley would be carted off in an ambulance, drugged to the hilt, and confined, for God only knew how long, in a locked facility.

It must not happen.

She had to act. And quickly!

Taking a cue from the woman's continuous stream of comments, she gathered her courage and walked toward the bed talking in a friendly, comforting voice with each cautious step.

"Louise, I am Hilary Dempster from Harmony House. I am so glad to find you here. Dennis let me in.

I just want to tell you how glad we are next door

that the whole mystery of the lights in the tower has been solved. It was Honor's young niece who climbed up there to get privacy for a school project. Oh, of course, you and I know she was wrong to take that risk but everything is fine now. We want you to come over and join us for a meal soon. We look forward to that."

Hilary continued in the same vein while watching to see the reaction. Louise stopped crying. She turned in amazement and seemed to recognize Hilary. The ghost of a smile crept across her tear-ravaged face and she reached out her hands toward Hilary.

The grip of those hands was something Hilary Dempster would never forget. It was the grip of a drowning person who is saved at the very last minute.

When the panic began to leave Louise's face and body, Hilary knew she had returned to some semblance of sanity and security. There was likely a long road ahead for her but a corner had been turned.

She continued to talk while she disentangled the damp hands. Then she slowly walked Louise to the adjoining washroom with a reassuring hand across her shoulders while she washed her face, tidied her hair and straightened her clothes.

The next hurdle was present in Hilary's mind while she continued to speak kindly to Louise. She must explain the arrival of the ambulance in such a way as to prevent Louise from dropping back into her manic state.

Thank God the ambulance has not yet arrived. It must have been delayed. How could that man leave his wife to this fate and go off to work?

When the first genuine, if shaky, smile dawned on Louise's face, Hilary began to walk her to the stairs talking all the way.

"Let's just go downstairs now, Louise. We both need a cup of tea to calm us down. I have to tell you something but I don't want you to worry. In a little while some nice men will arrive here. They want to help you. You know you have been unwell and it's best if you go to the hospital to be checked out and to get your medications fixed so you won't feel so desperate any longer. Do not be afraid, Louise. This is a good thing to do and I will be right with you all the way, holding your hand, just like I am now. We'll wait in the kitchen where I can see the front driveway. You boil some water for tea and I will watch for the nice men and talk to them first before they come inside.

Everything will be fine, you'll see. Everything will be better after this."

Hilary Dempster was making promises she could not be sure of keeping. It was breaking one of her most precious rules of conduct, but this situation demanded extraordinary action.

She had promised.

She made up her mind on the spot to fulfil those promises to the best of her ability. She would talk to the ambulance people first and explain that their patient was not as badly off as they had been led to believe. She would accompany Louise and see her settled after talking again to her doctor or psychiatrist or whomever was in charge at admissions. When all had been done at the hospital, she would track down one Dennis Ridley and beard him in his office, if necessary, and give him the lecture he so badly needed. Her opinion of the 'nice, friendly' man next door had taken a dive downward. She mentally ticked off the relevant points on a list.

Keeping his wife isolated from society was inimitable to her health.

Dozing her with pills was making her worse, not better.

Allowing a bad situation to get to this stage where such intervention was needed was reprehensible.

Not believing her concerns and letting Louise think she was crazy was ridiculous when a frank conversation with the inhabitants of Harmony House about his wife's concerns would have prevented a number of outcomes from developing.

There was more on the list but she saw the ambulance arriving. No sirens were being used.

Reassuring Louise once more, Hilary placed her hands around the cup of tea and told her to sip until she returned.

"I will be just a minute or two. Stay calm. All will be well, my dear. I will not leave you."

Hilary Dempster stood at her full, and impressive, height and prepared for battle. She would not permit the attendants to enter until they agreed to allow her to accompany Louise in the ambulance.

She knew what had to be said and done.

She would fight on behalf of this lonely woman, as she had fought for many a child in her years in education.

It felt rather good to be back in charge again with a clear mind and purpose.

CHAPTER 19

Thanksgiving in Canada falls in the middle of October. Mavis and Hilary had a meeting to decide how they would celebrate the holiday weekend.

"Such a lot has happened since summer. I believe it's time for a celebration. We'll do the turkey and all the trimmings. Eve is on board with that."

"I agree, Mavis. We need to take stock together. I think we should use the winter dining room for this occasion. Now, who should be invited to join us?"

This decision required another discussion. In the end the number came to ten.

"Can we seat that many?"

"I believe so. The extending section of my old

dining table is stored in the garage. We can bring chairs from the kitchen to make up the number."

"It will be quite the party, then. It's time to welcome our friends to our table."

"Most will be new friends but there's nothing wrong with that, is there?"

"Nothing wrong at all! It's a sign we are settling into our new lives at Harmony House.

I'll get started on the shopping list. Eve and I will shop with some advice from Faith about where best to go for bargains. Don't you think Faith has changed for the better since that tower incident was put behind her?"

"I am sure she has, but there's a reason. I'll let her tell you herself."

"Oh, a mystery? That should be interesting."

In fact, Hilary believed there would be more than one surprise around the Thanksgiving table and she was looking forward to all the revelations that would be shared. One advantage to being the person perceived to be 'in charge' at their mutual home, was that she was the recipient of all the secrets, both good and bad. She had finally begun to learn not to let this responsibility overwhelm her.

Her life was in far better balance these days. She had discovered most of the shared concerns were solved by the simple act of expressing them to another person. Of course there were more weighty issues, such as the matter of Louise Ridley and the poor decisions made by Faith Jeffries that had precipitated that particular crisis. The majority of issues were of the minor variety requiring only a listening ear.

And yet, she was looking forward to the revelations of this special occasion with happy anticipation. Not only because she had a hand in some of it, but also because it was a demonstration of how well the co-housing project was transitioning to something far beyond anything that could have been imagined in those first fraught months when Mavis and she commiserated privately about whether or not they had done the right thing in initiating the project.

This Thanksgiving meal would be the proof of the pudding, as they used to say. She chuckled at the play on words. The pudding, and all the other items that came together to make a great meal, would be a shared responsibility this year, with Eve coordinating the courses.

She started to plan the seating arrangement then realized there were several people who needed either a personal or a written invitation.

"That takes priority," she said, and with typical resolve she set about the task.

First she went to see Louise and Dennis. There was much to and fro between the houses since the desperate incident with the ambulance. So much so that Dennis, with Andy's help, had opened a passageway in the tree barrier so Hilary and Mavis had easier access.

The first difficult few hours with Dennis Ridley when she took him to task for his behaviour with Louise, were now in the past. Hilary still maintained close contact with Louise, even visiting her in the psychiatric ward, and with Mavis's support, taking Louise for outings around the Forks of the Thames where the sight of children playing happily in the fountains seemed to calm her mind remarkably.

Louise's progress had been rapid once her situation was understood. Dennis played his part in this recovery, with some urging from Hilary and Mavis. He underwent shock therapy of a kind when he realized how he had unwittingly contributed to his wife's deterioration by neglect of her needs.

Hilary learned Louise had once been a smart and efficient legal secretary. It was her husband who insisted she stay at home as a symbol to his business associates of how well he was prospering.

For some reason he got it into his head that men with stay-at-home wives were superior to others.

The original plan for Louise to have babies did

not work out and the situation was allowed to drift until the two were isolated in the house that was far too large for the needs of either of them.

"I can't thank you enough, Hilary. I know I did not welcome your intrusion into my private life, initially, and I apologize for my abruptness, but when I realized what you did to comfort and advise my wife; things *I* should have done for her, I used my guilt to amend my behaviour and my work schedules and everything else that came between us. When Louise returns home, all will be changed."

He was as good as his word. The proof was in Louise's demeanour. She smiled. She stood tall. She looked Mavis and Hilary in the face. She came over to Harmony House and took afternoon tea as she had dreamed of doing. She was welcomed by all. Vilma took her on a shopping expedition to buy a new wardrobe of fashionable clothes to suit her slim figure and also introduced her to the world of subtle make-up and hair styling.

A refreshed and energetic Louise now took particular interest in Eve's paintings. With very little encouragement, she tried the emotional release that Eve had discovered and painted wildly alongside her while Eve was working in her room.

Louise declared after these sessions, "I had no

idea how therapeutic art can be. I love splashing around the colours and seeing what comes to mind."

Dennis was happy to subsidize the materials required, and as it turned out colour became a theme in their renewal. Together they redecorated the master bedroom in a sunny yellow and organized the upper bedroom into an art studio where all the old fixations were painted into oblivion.

There was one other colour venture that brought a satisfied smile to Hilary's face every day.

When Dennis begged her to say what he could do to recompense her for all her help with Louise, Hilary immediately remembered the stair carpeting next door.

"Well, Dennis, my reward is to see how well you two are doing these days. But, if you insist, I would love it if you could arrange for someone to remove the gaudy purple carpeting from our hall staircase at Harmony House and replace it with a nice neutral colour, similar to your own choice."

This was, clearly, not what Dennis Ridley had expected to hear but he recovered swiftly and agreed to get this done with all speed before Thanksgiving.

"It's the very least I can do, Hilary. Without your intervention my life would be a shadow of what it now has become. I am at your service and the service of all at Harmony House, from now on. Just ask me."

Louise and Dennis would be invited to join the Harmony House family for Thanksgiving the next time she was in their home. Louise would be asked to contribute something to the feast and that would be the topic of their discussion.

Next on her list was the matter of approaching Vilma about the idea of including Andy this year. For one thing, Dennis would be more comfortable if another male was at the table.

For another, Andy Patterson had become an essential part of the co-housing project with respect to all things external around the property. Her observations of his interactions with Vilma and her dogs indicated he was becoming equally important in that sphere also. Mavis confirmed this, and it was decided to tackle Vilma as she returned from the dogs' morning exercise.

This was duly accomplished the next day. Hilary waited patiently while the dogs' feet were wiped and dried. She was happy to observe this routine, especially now that the new staircase carpet was likely to show the marks of eight paws and claws more readily.

"Just give me a minute to settle these two and I will join you in the kitchen, Hilary."

What Hilary did not know was how anxious Vilma was to talk about the fast-approaching Dog Show venture. Although she had already made up her mind to participate, it was something she wanted to run past Hilary for advice.

The matter of the Thanksgiving invitation was quickly settled over a cup of steaming hot coffee and Vilma used it as an introduction to her more pressing topic.

"Of course you have noticed how much time I spend with Andy at his farm. The dog training has advanced far beyond the basics now and I have agreed to accompany Andy to a Dog Show near Cornwall, Ontario, in a few weeks."

Hilary immediately realized this was a major expedition requiring one or, more likely, two overnight stays. She refrained from pointing to this delicate matter and applauded Vilma for her generosity of time and devotion to her dogs.

"Oscar and Astrid are remarkably disciplined animals for which both you and Andy are to be commended. I will admit I had some misgivings when you suddenly appeared with the dogs, but I know all of us welcome them for our own reasons. I am glad of the security aspect, for instance. No intruder would get far in this house without alerting those dogs of yours, Vilma.

Now, how do you feel about spending this amount of time in his company in a different environment from home?"

"Frankly, Hilary, I feel obliged to help Andy. He would like to reinvent himself as a dog trainer and doing well at a competition like this one would allow him to advertise his skills and set up a dog-handling business. He has not charged me for all the hours he devotes to my two and I know he has little money from his gardening and snow clearing routes. I mean to find a way to pay for this event out of town as a thank you."

"Good idea! The Thanksgiving meal invitation can be our way to begin to thank him for all he does at Harmony House. Now that you mention it, Vilma, I will do something about a regular payment for extra services here. I should have thought of it before this. We have been taking advantage of Andy.

But, my dear, you have not answered my question. What are your personal feelings toward Andy Patterson?"

This might be considered as stepping across a line and Hilary did not want to offend Vilma. She waited for the answer with some concern.

Vilma put down the large mug of coffee with

which she was unconsciously concealing the lower part of her face. Hilary had forced the issue and she must respond.

"It's very difficult for me. I swore never to let a man into my life again. Andy has not been intrusive; quite the opposite, in fact. He makes it perfectly clear how much he values his privacy.

I won't go into the story, but he has some traumatic events in his past that give him cause for reticence.

If anything, he has been the one pushing me away."

"So, not an easy man to know?"

"Exactly!"

"But that has given you time to appreciate his qualities, I think?"

"I suppose you are right. I feel differently about him each time he comes to my rescue in one way or another. I think that slow progress is probably a good thing. Certainly my other relationships with men have been much more of the fast and furious variety."

Both women chuckled at this description and the mood altered.

"Well, Vilma, it seems your association with Andy will come to a point of change at the Dog

Show, for better or ill. I will be interested to see how this works out for you."

"Me, too, Hilary! The family meal here will be a first step."

Conversation over a second cup of coffee turned to other matters until Vilma gave a start and announced, "I almost forgot. There's another issue with respect to this trip. I looked at the itinerary and it is likely we will stop overnight at Kingston to give the dogs, and us, a break from travelling.

Didn't Honor say Faith's supposed father lives in Kingston with his family? I was wondering if Faith would like to arrange to spend a weekend with them. Andy and I could pick her up on our return journey.

What do you think?"

"I think that's amazingly generous, even for you, Vilma. I thought you were not particularly keen on Faith.

"Correct! I am suspicious of teenagers in general, and she has proved me right more than once. However, I have to give the girl credit for the initiative she showed with the Finding Father business. I do not approve of the way she chose to do that, of course."

"I totally understand your feelings on that particular matter. Honor and I are determined to keep a tight rein on young Faith from now on and she has given us fervent promises to that end.

I suggest you talk to Honor about this. Don't mention it to Faith, of course. It would be a huge incentive for her if everyone involved agrees."

Vilma nodded. She thought there was another benefit to having Faith in her car during the long hours of driving. Conversation would be easier between the two females and Andy would be unable to introduce any personal topics.

Hilary felt she was doing well and receiving positive responses. She wanted to continue with the good momentum but she needed time to recover.

Eve entered the kitchen just as Vilma departed and offered to make an omelette or scrambled eggs.

It was exactly what Hilary needed and provided an opportunity to discuss the Thanksgiving meal plans.

Breakfast was shared and the plans advanced.

Eve suggested special family recipes should be included.

"Every family seems to have one special dessert, or dish of stuffing, or vegetables that represents Thanksgiving to them. It would be fun to incorporate those dishes and makes the conversation around the table flow with good memories."

"I love that idea, Eve! This will be such a lovely evening. We'll ask the men to pour wine. It will be rather nice to have some male company at the table for a change."

Later in the afternoon, Hilary went downstairs to talk to Honor before Faith arrived home from school.

She found Honor flat on the floor and was alarmed for a moment until she realized she was doing yoga exercises while watching a video on her computer screen.

"Oh, Honor, I don't want to interrupt. I can come back later."

"No, Hilary. Almost done. Just a last stretch or two. Sit down, please."

It was interesting to see Honor work through the stretches. She was much more flexible than when she first arrived at Harmony House. It occurred to Hilary that the office space could be used as a sort of yoga studio. With winter fast approaching an indoor exercise program could be of benefit to more than one of the women. It was another example of the multiple ways the house could adapt to their needs.

She would broach the subject with Mavis and Eve and see what they thought. Honor would be an excellent guide to yoga if what she now saw was typical of her skill level.

"My goodness, Honor! That last position was quite difficult. How long have you been doing this?"

"Several months now. I decided to improve my overall health now my hip is comfortable. It's amazing how it helps brain and body to be more fit."

"Very impressive! Well done! A good example for the rest of us women."

Honor blushed to the roots of her red hair, which Hilary noticed was now a more subdued shade of auburn rather than the previous, rather glaring red. It seemed Honor was making more than one change. Faith's presence could be having an effect on her aunt in positive ways. It was a good thing. Keeping an eye on the activities of one Faith Jeffries demanded all the brain and body fitness that could be obtained. She was a challenge all right but her arrival had, undoubtedly, brought a breath of youth and vitality to their home.

Honor rolled up her yoga mat and wiped her face with a towel before fetching a glass of mineral water from her mini fridge. "May I get you something, Hilary?"

"No thank you. I won't take a minute of your

time. I have a proposition for Faith, courtesy of an offer from Vilma, but I need to know if it would be something you think Faith wants to do."

"Sounds intriguing!"

Honor slipped a sweater over her shoulders and composed herself to receive this news.

"I remember you saying that Jar Jeffries, I mean *Mason,* of course, invited Faith to visit his family in Kingston. It turns out that Vilma and Andy are driving out of town in November to an event. They will pass through Kingston and stay there overnight. It's a chance for Faith to meet up with Mason and that child of his, Melvin, who was instrumental in connecting the two.

Vilma assures me she would take Faith there and stay long enough to make sure everything is comfortable for Faith with respect to facilities like accommodations. I understand there are three young boys in the family.

I need you to talk to Faith and see if this is amenable to her. If so, the Jeffries would require to be notified about the dates and so on."

Honor looked thoughtful. She folded the arms of her sweater across her chest in a loose knot.

"The last time Faith mentioned the Jeffries she suggested the whole business was finished and done with. Of course, she did not foresee an opportunity like this.

Leave it with me, Hilary. I will find the right time to ask her. She is, as you know, keeping very busy with school projects. This break might be good for her in several ways."

"I'll leave it in your capable hands then. It could be something interesting to share at Thanksgiving if it all works out."

"Indeed!"

CHAPTER 20

"I suppose it's too early to bring a potted Christmas tree indoors like we did last year?"

"If you want the poor thing to dry out completely, it is, but I have another idea."

Mavis and Hilary stood in the foyer, planning the program for the big Thanksgiving dinner. It seemed appropriate to spend time on the appearance of the house entrance. It was the first thing their visitors would see when they arrived. Hilary was particularly anxious to showcase the area now that the stairs were carpeted in beautiful new fabric of a neutral colour.

"I was thinking we could find a fragrant bush like lavender or rosemary. I still have some nice, large pots in the garage storage. We could set the potted plant up on the hall table with a fall bouquet or pumpkin, similar to the one we'll place in the centre of the dining table."

"Should we have candles?"

"Absolutely! But not out here! We need to keep an eye on them. What about a collection of smaller candle holders in the dining room? We don't want anything too tall to block sightlines across the table."

"I'll get started on that right away, Mavis."

"One more thing; I was thinking we should have a reception with drinks and snacks before we go into the dining room."

"That would be elegant, but the kitchen will be too busy with preparations for serving. We will all take a turn of serving and clearing so there must be space left for coming and going."

"Correct! I wondered if we could kill two birds with one stone, as it were. What about holding our reception in the former guest suite?"

"Oh my! I see what you mean. It's the perfect place, but Faith would need to vacate after doing a massive clean-up first. Once the bed is folded up, there's plenty of floor space......"

"....and the piano could be played, Mavis. Wouldn't that be a lovely welcome?"

"I suppose I could practise a few pieces for the occasion."

"Excellent! It's all coming together perfectly. We will give Faith a hand with the cleaning and we'll spring it on her soon, so she has time to hide anything personal from view.

Will Marble mind being ousted for a few hours?"

"She will be happy in my quiet tower room far from the hustle and bustle, don't worry."

The mention of the word 'tower' gave Hilary another festive idea which she meant to discuss with Andy.

If she could persuade him to do the ladder climb, up to the top of the tower, and place in there a large lantern with a battery, the light would send out a glow to suit the season of goodwill. It might last for weeks, possibly until Christmas, and Andy would not need to remove it when the battery ran out.

By Thanksgiving Sunday, Harmony House was ready. There was an air of excitement, combined with delicious smells and the rustle of dresses and skirts since the women had decided it was an occasion deserving of their best attire.

Honor had taken Faith shopping for a long skirt and lacy top and the outfit added inches to her height, assisted by her first heels and a hairstyle consisting of curls piled loosely on top of her head.

Honor used the opportunity to buy a smart dress in a size and colour she had never dared to wear before. When aunt and niece admired their finished look together, in a long mirror, there was, for the first time, a resemblance between them that had nothing to do with hair or clothes but more to do with the pleased expressions on their faces.

Jannice borrowed an older dress of Vilma's which she had saved because it had good memories of Nolan attached to it.

"It's too small for me now, Jannice, but the proportions are exactly right for you and the mid-calf length suits you well."

"What a lovely thing! I feel like a princess with the skirt swishing around my legs and the deep V neckline. It's not too revealing is it?"

"Not at all! You should show off your assets, my dear. That shade of pale green brings out your fine complexion and the depth of your dark, shining hair. I will never wear this again, so it's yours."

"Oh, I couldn't accept that! It's too much!"

As Jannice's lips pronounced this objection, her eyes were glowing. She studied her reflection in the long mirror in Vilma's washroom. Her hands gently smoothed the rich fabric around her waist and she swung her hips to see the effect of the folds of skirt wafting about her legs.

Vilma knew she adored the dress. She knew if it was to be worn again to create more good memories, there was no one else to whom she would rather gift it. In her heart she hoped for other suitable occasions for Jannice to enjoy the dress.

"See how you feel after the dinner tonight. I think you will vote to keep it, Jannice. It was always a lucky dress for me."

Hilary and Mavis retrieved dressy clothes from the downstairs storage lockers and gave Honor a preview.

"Oh, I do like that navy blue outfit on you, Hilary. It's smart and not too fussy.

Mavis, your brocade skirt and jacket are elegant and timeless, and if you have a white blouse with a bow or ruffle at the neck it will set off the patterns nicely.

You both look ready. Just run the clothes in the dryer for a minute or two to remove any wrinkles from being folded and you are good to go."

Hilary surmised Honor had been paying more

attention to clothes since Faith came on the scene. The girl's school outfits seemed strange to the older woman but Honor assured her she was right in style for the teen scene. Apparently, Faith bought her own school clothes, in consultation with her friends, using her own money from part-time jobs.

Honor had learned a lot from listening to how this was done. Faith had shown her Instagram photos of how the most fashionable kids were dressing these days. The styles were individual, for the most part, and that was what appealed to the kids.

Hilary decided this was better than the false conformity of uniforms such as she was subjected to in her high school years.

Eve debated about what to wear. She really owned nothing suitable and could not afford to buy clothes that might never be worn more than once. Despite this, she thought it was time to make her mark.

She had come through a very difficult time and emerged intact. It was something to celebrate and she wanted to do that in style.

She and Honor had discussed this very matter one day over coffee. Eve learned about fabric production methods because of a client of Honor's who offered innovative online clothing.

"What they do is provide a service producing clothing printed with art or designs submitted by their

customers. I'll show you some of their products."

Eve was duly impressed and the idea had lingered in her mind.

What if she photographed one of her favourite flower paintings and had it reproduced on a pair of slim pants and a vest? The company advertised a Lycra fabric which would stretch for comfort if she got the measurements wrong.

With Honor's help, the order was placed and the finished work arrived in due course, to the satisfaction of both women.

"This is beautiful, and completely unique, Eve! It's yours in every possible way.

You should think of producing more items incorporating your paintings."

Once again, Honor's words had an effect. The result was an announcement that Eve planned to make at the Thanksgiving dinner table.

Dusk was falling as Louise and Dennis Ridley

walked, arm in arm, through the break in their greenery to Harmony House.

There was a moment of hesitation when Louise noticed the glow of a lamp from the top of the tower and remembered the impact on her life of a smaller light up there. The moment passed by when Dennis spoke.

"Isn't that a charming effect, Louise! The golden glow will get brighter as darkness falls and light our way home later."

Sensing her momentary discomfort, he pulled her arm closer to his chest and smiled reassuringly.

"I hope you are looking forward to this evening as much as I am, my darling. That vegetable dish you sent over earlier, smelled delicious. I can hardly wait to sink my teeth into it."

"Well, you are in for several treats if the display of foods I saw laid out in their kitchen is any indication."

She breathed out, relaxed as she had been taught, and smiled up at her handsome husband.

"How nice to be going there together, Dennis. The women have been so welcoming to me. I can't explain what a difference they have made to my life."

He nodded and squeezed her arm. He would never be able to adequately thank Hilary Dempster for her intervention. The business with the carpeting that had startled him at first, was only the beginning of what he intended to be a mutually-beneficial association. He had a life-changing project he would discuss soon with Mavis and Hilary before talking to Louise, but tonight was all about fellowship and appreciation and he was in a good mood for both.

The sounds of a piano drifted over to them as soon as Hilary opened the front door with a welcoming smile. "Hello there! Please let me take your coats and go ahead into the reception room for drinks and snacks. Faith is serving and Mavis is our pianist. Jannice, Vilma and Honor are already there and we are waiting for Andy to arrive."

Everyone turned to greet the new arrivals and a party atmosphere was immediately evident.

Soon Louise and Dennis had drinks in hand and were admiring the light and airy room with its expanse of pale carpet and comfy sofa. The music in the background filled any gaps in conversation until Eve appeared to announce she had seen Andy's truck arriving.

Vilma went out to greet him and saw he had made quite an effort as far as attire was concerned. She had never before seen him in formal clothes. This dark suit looked new and its clean lines were set off by a pale blue shirt and matching tie with a tiny print. His hair was freshly combed back from his forehead and his tan appeared deeper in contrast to the pale shirt.

Vilma was taken aback at this new version of Andy Patterson. She thought he would not look out of place at a formal event anywhere. She was reminded for the first time, of his former career as a uniformed policeman. Divested of the tools of his gardening job, he stood taller and more confident. She accompanied him into the reception with a sense of pride.

Andy was struck at once by Vilma Smith, the elegant and exquisite lady, in a dress that shaded from lavender at her bare shoulders, to deep purple at her feet. Gone was the sporty look she favoured when with her dogs. This transformation revealed a beautiful figure and stylish hairstyle.

He was speechless. He hoped a tremulous smile and a raised eyebrow spoke to her of his surprise and delight.

What is this gorgeous creature doing with me? How am I going to get through this evening without taking my eyes off her?

A few minutes later, once Andy had acquired a drink and exchanged casual conversation, the party advanced to the winter dining room.

Some discussion about the seating arrangement

had taken place prior to this occasion. The final decision placed Hilary and Mavis at either end of the table with the two men opposite each other in the middle seats, and Vilma and Louise beside their partners. Eve insisted on sitting to Mavis's left which put her nearest to the exit and closer to the kitchen. Honor chose to sit beside Andy with Faith on her other side. She thought it might well be necessary to quietly advise her niece at this, her first grown-up dinner.

There were several gasps of delight when the guests entered the dining room. The gas fire was lit, the chandelier over the table cast light onto bright candles, gleaming glasses and polished silverware and the Thanksgiving centrepiece, a masterly concoction of seasonal leaves, berries and fruits drew all eyes and added its own outdoor scents to compete with male aftershave and female perfumes.

Hilary gave a sigh of relief. She had been ordered to remain in position and allow the others to serve and remove plates. When she protested, Mavis reminded her she would be in charge of keeping the conversation going during any interruptions. She was also charged with gathering intel for later discussion. As Hilary already knew some of the previously-secret bombshells to be thrown at this event she wisely agreed to take on these responsibilities.

To reduce the number of interruptions, Eve planned to arrange hot dishes from the kitchen along the sideboard credenza, protecting the polished wood by placing a long, many-folded tablecloth on its surface. From here, dishes could be circulated and returned. As there were a number of special side dishes for the main course, this was a good plan. The turkey, partially dismembered on its huge platter, would be placed in front of Hilary since she had the most experience in carving meat.

Before the main part of the meal commenced, with salads dispensed and wine poured by Dennis, a toast was made by Mavis.

"Welcome everyone to our feast. We at Harmony House have so much for which we are truly thankful in this beautiful season when we take a break and think of our blessings. Please join hands around the table and take turns expressing one thing in your life that is new and good. I'll begin.

I am glad to have survived long enough to see this table full of friendly faces!"

Mavis's humour set the tone and everyone knew it was not intended to be a chore to think of something profound and original.

Eve followed on by saying she cherished her painting.

Louise hesitated, then looked around the table and simply said she valued every person here, while Dennis underlined her comment and called them all prime rescuers.

Jannice said she would need an hour to list her true blessings, and that in itself is a good thing.

Hilary beamed, and stated everyone around the table had taught her many valuable lessons this year. Vilma brought laughter by adding her dogs gave her a new lease on life and insight into how people and animals are similar in their basic needs.

Andy was grateful for a few seconds to prepare. He cleared his throat and said life was full of unexpected twists and turns and the Harmony House inhabitants had given him the new beginning he badly needed.

Honor was temporarily overcome with emotion and quickly announced her new and good item was sitting to her left which caused an audible 'ah' to circulate.

Faith was thinking along similar lines, but did not want to repeat her aunt's statement so she simply said, "I never knew what family meant until I entered this home. Family can be those to whom you are related." At this point she squeezed Honor's hand hard. "It can also be those who open their hearts to you in love and acceptance. Thank you."

There was a brief silence while throats were cleared. Then hands were dropped and applause filled the room to Hilary's cry of ….. "Now, Happy Thanksgiving to all of us and let the feasting commence!"

It was a memorable night, not least for the amount of good food consumed with relish. The hot dishes were placed on the credenza, emptied, and returned to the kitchen on a tray, to be replaced with more. Conversation flowed easily as family recipes were discussed and their merits assessed.

It was not until the selection of desserts, from pies to tiny pastries and fruits, had been sampled, that the room settled down over coffee and mints for more serious matters.

Honor took the lead.

"I am proud to announce to all of you, an accomplishment of my niece, Faith. She is working on a school assignment consisting of a journal and accompanying internet project. I believe most of you know about the unusual internet part of this, but there is a recent development. Faith's teacher has asked her to be an ambassador for mental health.

She has already given a speech to her school assembly about the trials of her early life and what she has learned from these. The speech was so well received that she will be speaking to other London schools in the near future. This accomplishment will contribute to the community service portion of her secondary school studies."

Spontaneous applause broke out and Faith was inundated with genuine praise which almost brought her to tears despite knowing about the announcement beforehand and steeling herself for it.

Vilma took up the theme. "Faith will be travelling part of the way with Andy, myself, and the dogs, to an Agility and Obedience trial in Long Sault in a few weeks. Faith will stop off in Kingston to visit with the young boy who put her in touch again with the man who was an important part of her early life."

"This is amazing news, Vilma! Congratulations to all three of you, and the dogs, of course. That will be very exciting all round. I hope Faith will work ahead to justify the time off school."

Faith chirped up in reply to Hilary's comment. "Don't worry! It's all been approved and it will be a part of my assignment. Oh, I almost forgot! *Please* no birthday gifts for me this year. I have everything I need."

When the questions had subsided, Jannice looked over at Vilma for reassurance and got the nod of the head she needed to continue.

"Well, now! I have a trip of my own to announce, but it's not until later in the year.

You see, I will be absent over most of Christmas as I have been invited back to my old home to share the celebration with the new owners. Then I will be going to Quebec City where a gentleman called Mitchell Delaney, who some of you have met, is interviewing me for a book on old Irish tales and history."

This was news to most around the table and it was the last thing they expected to hear from Jannice O'Connor, arguably the most reserved, and least adventurous, of all of them.

Many were thinking back to the subdued little person they had first met in Camden Corners. Mavis and Hilary looked to Vilma who they held responsible for these changes in her protégé. Vilma just smiled, somewhat like a proud mother whose child has become independent.

"Goodness me! Are there any more exciting events to be announced tonight?" Mavis looked around the table. She bypassed Dennis. His secret idea was not yet ready for public consumption.

This time Honor placed Eve on centre stage by

saying, "There's someone who has been busy with food most of the evening but who deserves her own acclaim for that, and a further example of her accomplishments. Tell us about it, Eve."

That lady simply stood and displayed her outfit by turning around and back again.

"This garment has been designed and made to my specifications from one of my paintings. Thanks to the internet skills of Honor Pace here, there is a new website, called 'Eve's Garden' where anyone can buy clothing like this. On the mantelpiece you can help yourself to a flyer with additional information and styles."

She sat down to more applause and congratulations. Hilary who had earlier commented on Eve's new outfit had not been told the secret, and she was astonished to think of how much progress this woman had made in emerging from her self-imposed shell of darkness and depression.

Hilary summarized for all of them. "What a night this is! So much to talk about!

Please sit at the table with more coffee or go to the fireplace, or retire to the reception room if you wish. Eve and I will be clearing the dishes but the evening is by no means over. Just relax and talk together."

Faith jumped up. She had had enough of sitting under intense inspection and she began to pile up the empty dishes on the credenza with the plan to take these to the kitchen and stay there, washing dishes if necessary, until the guests had left and she could resume her occupation of the former guest suite.

She had a sudden thought. *Have I left anything incriminating in the washroom?*

She searched her memory but could not come up with anything in particular. One or two cosmetic items were lying on the floor of the shower with a waterproof box holding her phone and journal. Mavis had made sure there were fresh towels folded properly on the rails and the air had been sprayed with a scented aerosol for guest use. All was secure for the remainder of the evening.

She could not wait to tell the gang about this, her first ever Thanksgiving at which she had something special of her own to celebrate.

CHAPTER 21

The ripples from the Thanksgiving dinner at Harmony House were to spread far and wide in the following months. It seemed as if the formal announcements gave impetus to the various projects that had been going on in comparative secrecy.

Jannice began assembling photographs and anecdotes from her family history, including the beautiful pictures of her wearing the antique gowns discovered locked in the attic wardrobe.

Eve continued painting and searched for a venue in which her latest art work could receive a wider audience.

Honor monitored the clothing production for Eve's Garden and arranged the distribution of garments through a delivery company, with payments going to Eve's account via Pay Pal.

Faith kept up communications with the Kingston family and grew closer to Melvin and his mother, Pauline, which gave her some assurance that a weekend with them was not going to be unbearable.

She worried a bit when Vilma revealed it was a seven hour car journey to the Dog Show location, but relaxed when she remembered she was not going all the way. She did, however decide to spend a bit of time with Vilma's dogs after she figured out the back seat of the car was likely to be crowded and she would be crammed between the animals. The last thing she wanted was to arrive in Kingston with blood dripping from dog bites.

Vilma became increasingly glad she would have Faith in the car for part of the journey. She planned to ask her about her school presentations and what she had observed as a result. It would be a nice change to be able to talk to a teenager who was doing something to help others instead of fixating on appearances or thinking up ways to annoy the life out of a stepmother.

The day of departure drew near very quickly. Andy

was busy with Fall gardening chores and extra practices with the dogs. Vilma made sure her car was in peak condition and set aside everything the dogs would need for their comfort both on the trip, and in the hotel.

She was determined to find a way to fund the expenses and she began to manage this after Andy revealed where he had made a hotel reservation. She researched the Long Sault Motel online and discovered it rated only two stars and cost $65 per night. The location was certainly handy for the dog show but she quickly found a Best Western Inn, two minutes from downtown Cornwall with luxury suites, good pub food, fridge in the room and, best of all, it was dog friendly, supplying doggie cookies and treats. She made reservations for two expensive, large suites that were still vacant and paid up front. She knew she might have to insist the first hotel was not suitable for her and the dogs and make a play of finding another for them.

She would make sure the blame for the change of plan was all hers, and, therefore, she must compensate Andy for his out-of-pocket expenses. This move would put her safely in the driver's seat regarding what was to be spent for their comfort in the second hotel.

With these two issues settled in her mind she

began to assemble her clothes and necessities. She was committed to this expedition and she would do her best to get through it without too much stress. After all, it was to be her last serious connection with Andy Patterson. She would be as pleasant as possible. After they returned to London she intended to draw a halt to the dog training.

~

They set off early on the Friday morning to avoid heavy traffic on the 401. Vilma was driving, with Andy monitoring the road conditions and looking for alternative routes using Vilma's smartphone.

Driving through Toronto was always stressful but they took the fast route and paid the toll. Once outside the city they were closer to Lake Ontario and farmland. Here, Andy took over the driving and soon became accustomed to handling the large car with its automatic transmission.

Conversation had been limited to this point. In the rear seats, Faith had fallen asleep with two heavy, warm paws in her lap. She did not wake until they drew into a Service Centre and Vilma released the dogs to run around in an area set aside for that purpose. Andy and Faith went into the restaurant and scoped out the offerings, returning with hot food in containers. Vilma had water and chews for the dogs and they sat down at an outdoor picnic table away from the car parking and enjoyed what there was of November sunshine with coat collars turned up against the wind, and hands wrapped around hot drinks. Andy finished eating and went off with Astrid and Oscar for some obedience training.

"How are you managing in the back seat, Faith? It's not too cramped for you?"

"It's fine! The dogs are like big furry blankets. Other than licking my hands a lot they have let me sleep. Oh, I washed my hands in the washroom inside, in case you are worried."

Vilma chuckled. She also washed frequently when the dogs were being affectionate.

"Well, it won't be much longer now. The worst is over. Next big stop is in Kingston. How do you feel about that part? I promise you need not stay if you don't feel comfortable with the Jeffries' family."

"I'll be okay. I feel like I know them now. Melvin's mother is the boss and she has been very nice on the phone. She's giving me a room of my own for the weekend."

"That sounds good. You can call me if you have any concerns at all. We'll be staying overnight at a motel and I'll be doing nothing most of the time at the Dog Show. I can come and fetch you if you want."

"I'm pretty sure that won't be necessary but thanks for the thought. It will be different for me with three young boys in the house. Likely their mom will need help with them."

"You should also spend time with Mason Jeffries. I am sure you two have a lot of catching up to do."

Faith had thought about this part and decided to whitewash much of her childhood with Felicity. It would do no good to make Mr. Jeffries feel worse about abandoning them than he did already.

She realized now that he was not in love, or even in like, with her Mom. It was a business arrangement, made out of necessity and not a lifetime commitment. In many ways Mason was lucky to have escaped when he did. Jolene told her this was a very mature attitude to have. Faith meant to maintain it as much as possible. It was only two days.

Despite her optimism, Faith grew nervous when they arrived in Kingston, took a quick tour around the town by the lake and drove right out again to a subdivision some distance away.

Using her phone, Faith had called ahead to warn them she was near and they found the entire family waiting on the doorstep for her arrival.

The youngest boy was in his mother's arms. The next one up was holding onto his dad's hand and Melvin was standing tall on his own as if the whole deal was his idea; which it certainly was.

Vilma got out of the car and introduced herself to the parents. She explained that Andy would take the dogs for a short walk while she saw Faith settled, and then they must leave for their motel downtown.

Pauline invited her inside for a minute while Melvin helped Faith with her bag. Mason rustled up the kids and followed his wife to allow Andy to get the dogs out of the car. The younger boys want to pet the dogs when they saw them looking out of the window but Mason knew they were working dogs and not to be messed with. *Maybe later, after the Dog Show event when everybody is more relaxed.*

Vilma did a quick assessment of the modest house and praised Pauline for her lovely home, knowing the unspoken comment that it was wonderful how she coped with all these kids, was fully understood.

The two women had an immediate connection and Vilma was content to leave Faith in Pauline's more-than-capable hands.

Faith hung back until Vilma took her leave. She and Melvin had started to talk as soon as they opened up the trunk of the car. He was just as verbal as she expected and she was not surprised when his mother told him to show their guest to her room and where everything, meaning the washroom, was located.

It was a tiny room with a single bed but all was spotlessly clean and tidy.

"It's my room, usually, but it's yours now. I will be next door with Jason if you need me. Dad says come downstairs when you're ready. I've to leave you here for now. I'll be waiting for you. Bye Faith!"

She thought he looked and sounded like a nice little old man you might see in the park feeding the birds.

Could he really be just eight years old?

As for Mason Jar? She still called him this inside her head and it made this older man with the family responsibilities that had freaked him out some twelve years ago, more approachable. She honestly could see nothing in his appearance that was familiar. Could be, some turn of speech or physical habit might remind her but it was possible the old Jar was gone. She considered that was a good thing. She would start over with this man and see where, if anywhere, it could lead. In any case, a couple of days with Melvin were enough to keep her amused and she suspected Pauline was a pretty special mother worth watching.

She opened the bedroom door and found Melvin lounging, in what he assumed was a casual fashion, against the wall.

"So, come on down for supper. Ignore the little kids. Their eating habits are disgusting. After, we can go to my basement studio where all the neat stuff is. Dad will help show you my experiments. He's a scientist, you know."

Aha! A science nut! That makes sense. His room is full of models and posters. This is going to be a fast intro to the dad and little brother I never had.

❦

Vilma's decision to take over the accommodations for the Dog Show was proved right when she saw the motel Andy had chosen for their overnight in Kingston. It was a small place near an exit from the highway and close to a fast-food burger outlet. It was poorly furnished but her room had two single beds and at least the dogs would be sleeping up off the floor. Once glance at the condition of the carpet made her determined not to put a bare foot on it, no matter what.

Andy went off to get them some food while she unpacked the dogs' home comforts from the trunk of her car and was grateful they had their usual excellent dry food to eat. She inspected the washroom and estimated she could wash hands and face at the sink and clean her teeth but that would have to do until she reached the superior suite at the Best Western Hotel.

The dogs were restless after so many hours cooped up in the car and Andy was in a hurry to take them to a big field behind the motel and away from the road traffic zooming by on the highway.

Vilma thanked him politely for the milkshake and burger with fries, and disposed of most of it in the washroom bin as soon as he was out of sight. She turned back the cover over the bed and sat on the sheets and watched television for a few minutes until Andy returned with the dogs.

"I think we should get an early start," he said. "Once we are settled in the motel near Long Sault I must give the dogs a thorough run through of their training points so they will be ready for the obedience competition on Saturday afternoon."

Vilma had not planned to spring the change of accommodation on him this soon, but she thought it better to get that part over with so he would be in a calm frame of mind for the competition.

"Andy, I have to confess I am not happy with staying in motels like this. I have made reservations in a far superior place near Cornwall with luxury suites and dog friendly facilities. I hope you will not be angry about this. It's only fair if I pay my way. You are doing all of this for my dogs. You, and they, should be comfortable and well rested."

She watched his reaction with some trepidation. He took in a breath and bit his inner cheeks. He was clearly grappling with the circumstances that made it evident he was not able to supply what she was used to. It was a matter of pride. But he could not afford pride.

"I see. Well, an even earlier start is required. I need to stop at the Long Sault motel and cancel the rooms before heading into Cornwall. Be ready at six o'clock."

He was gone. The dogs crowded near her, knowing there was tension in the room. She stroked them with reassuring words and breathed a deep sigh. The worst was over now. When the competition ended on Sunday night she would pack up, check on the car and look forward to heading home. Faith had already kept the personal conversation to a minimum in the car. When the return journey was over, this connection to Andy Patterson would also be over. Forever.

CHAPTER 22

T he big conference hotel was exactly as Vilma had hoped. There was a large and luxurious double bed, a fireplace with a dog-sized soft rug in front, ample space in a well-appointed ensuite washroom and also a superb restaurant, as well as bar food on demand.

Andy did not comment about his matching suite. He took the dogs and the car and went off to the convention centre where the Agility and Obedience trials were being held. Several hours had been set aside for participants to exercise their dogs in the arena before the formal competition began.

Vilma enjoyed a long, hot bath and ordered room service. By the afternoon she was restored and revived and ready for whatever a dog show involved.

As soon as they reached the location it was obvious how popular this event was. Parked cars and vans stretched around the convention area and Vilma could see no spaces. Andy had acquired a competitor's parking badge in the morning and this permitted them to move close to the building.

It was all a new experience for Vilma but Andy was right at home and took over immediately.

"You should find a seat up high enough so you can see the entire arena floor. Collect some snacks inside. This will be a long session. Sit on your coat. This is usually a hockey centre and the benches are pretty hard."

She gave Astrid and Oscar a big hug and watched Andy lead them off to the competitors' entrance.

She had her phone with her and if things got boring she planned to watch a movie on Netflix using earbuds.

This plan dissipated as soon as she entered the building. The foyer was full of tables and displays related to everything canine. Cages of dogs were set around the floor and owners seemed to be spending time on brushing and grooming their animals to a high degree.

Vilma passed on through as quickly as possible only to find the actual competition area was even busier. The noise level was incredible. Barking dogs everywhere, a loud-speaker system tuning up for later announcements and an arena floor divided up into sections so the competitors and their dogs could walk through a series of typical contest challenges.

There were dogs of every shape and size, not to mention the number of dog handlers who either matched or contrasted with their pets. It was all new and extremely interesting to see. The level of excitement grew perceptibly, and the audience chattered about their favoured dogs and their hopes for success until the arena was ordered to be cleared of all competitors and the sand swept for the first group in the obedience section.

The announcer now took over and spoke only when some explanation was required. The obedience trials began with smaller dogs so Vilma could see what was expected. The judges stood in the centre with clipboards in hand and watched intently. Handlers were expected to demonstrate control by hand signals. The dog must stop on command, run, turn, sit, bark and do all this while another dog had started to perform. There was always something to watch and Vilma noticed the audience sighed in satisfaction when some particularly cute and clever animal performed a special trick. No applause was allowed and no judging announcements until the entire section had been completed.

Vilma began to get excited to see her dogs arrive, but she had to wait until mid-sized dogs were announced. As Andy entered with Oscar, it occurred to her to wonder where Astrid was waiting. Then she saw how well trained her dogs were. Only Oscar was entered in this part of the competition. Astrid was instructed to sit and stay to the side while Andy walked the route. She did this perfectly, and Vilma felt a surge of pride. Oscar did everything as required and finished with a nice flourish, rising onto his back legs and bowing his head to the audience. This received a well-deserved sigh of appreciation.

She sat through the large dog trials and found them less interesting. The dogs were slower and more awkward, she thought. She preferred the sparky personalities and swift movements of her Australians.

Hours had gone by. The line of dogs and handlers seemed endless. Vilma glanced at her phone and saw it was late in the evening. No one had left the seats. When the announcer asked for the floor to be cleared for the judges' decisions, a hush fell.

The judges were now seated beside the microphone. Vilma gathered up her coat and purse ready to exit. She badly needed a hot meal and a drink but there was no way to leave until the last words had been spoken. She estimated the crowd would not be pleased at any interruption at this stage in the proceedings.

Dogs and their handlers were summoned to receive certificates of excellence but Vilma could not perceive the difference between one or another of the competing dogs. The finer points escaped her.

She was not really listening until she heard 'Andrew Patterson and Oscar'.

My Oscar won something! Really?

She sat up straight to get a better view and saw Andy go forward to the judges to accept the certificate.

She wanted to turn around to the people seated behind her and say, "That's my dog!" but as no one else was making such comments, she suppressed the idea.

The announcements continued until all the winners were asked to make a circuit of the arena floor for applause. She waited and held her excitement until Andy and Oscar entered and then she stood and cheered and did not care if anyone disapproved.

The exodus from the arena took an age but at last she reached the car and found Andy and two dogs waiting.

"That was just so exciting! I was amazed to see Oscar perform and Astrid was such a good girl to wait at the side. When does she get a turn Andy?"

"Astrid is the star performer tomorrow at the Agility trials although Oscar will get his chance also.

Let's get out of here and back to the hotel. The dogs need some free play now. I must say, Vilma, the hotel you chose is very comfortable and the facilities for dogs are excellent.

Do you want to meet for a meal in an hour or so? We can discuss the day's activities."

She was happy to do this. After a quiet hour by the fire with a pot of tea she would be ready for anything and by then the dogs would be sleeping soundly.

She did not expect to find Andy wearing a more relaxed version of the outfit in which he appeared at the Thanksgiving meal in Harmony House. Since leaving London he had been in his usual jeans and sweater. She was surprised, but glad she had also changed into a simple knit top and skirt.

Andy chose the restaurant rather than the bar,

and they had a nice table near a window from where they could see people arriving all the time.

"This is a popular place to stay," she offered, as a conversation starter.

"I recognize some of the participants from this afternoon. The hotel is full of dog fans."

"I had no idea this kind of thing was so popular. It was quite a display today and I must congratulate you, Andy, on the job you did with Oscar. Was that little bow he performed a winning stroke?"

They were safely into the realm of dog talk and Andy had no trouble pointing out the finer details of a good performance. He removed and unrolled the certificate from his jacket pocket and showed it to her.

"Very handsome! This will look good in your barn when you open your training facility. That's still the plan, I presume?"

He hesitated for a few seconds before answering.

"It all depends on tomorrow's results. I need a big win to get accreditation and find clients willing to trust their animals to me. Publicity counts in this business."

"Are there not many other shows like this one, closer to home?"

"Yes, but not all of them count equally. This is

one of the big ones leading to competitions in the United States."

Their food arrived. It gave Vilma a chance to conceal her dismay at his comments. She did not want her dogs going all over the place without her. The sooner Andy established his business and had new client dogs, the better, as far as she was concerned. Suddenly, the results of tomorrow's test of dog agility assumed far more importance than she had expected.

CHAPTER 23

Andy slept as well as he could. The room was possibly too luxurious. It was the kind of thing his ex-wife would appreciate. He was more accustomed to Spartan accommodations. The bed seemed to engulf him and he was dreaming strange dreams about failure and its consequences.

He rose early and took a cool shower. There was milk in the small fridge so he made coffee and sat drinking it while he ran over in his mind the routine with the dogs. It all depended on their mood today.

So far, there had been no incidents to disrupt their concentration but one angry outbreak between competing animals could set up a chain of reactions and the control he needed would vanish like the early morning mist outside his bedroom window.

The holding area at the arena was well monitored on Saturday. He pinned his hopes on that situation being repeated today. So much depended on this day. He had told Vilma the truth when he said how much he was counting on a victory but he concealed part of the reason, as he had always concealed the inner functions of his mind and emotions when he was with her. It was an ingrained habit now, and he had no idea how to move from his present guarded position to one of more openness.

He allowed himself a few seconds to recall how wonderful it was to sit beside her in the restaurant last evening. It felt like a normal couple sharing a meal in a nice setting. The only difference was the conclusion of the evening when they went to separate rooms for the night.

It had taken him a very long time to acknowledge he wanted much more from Vilma Smith. He knew it was not likely she would ever climb down from her high horse and see him as he wanted to be seen.

He was totally to blame for this. He had shown her only the worst of himself.

He retreated behind his security barriers whenever she approached.

He made excuses for his cowardice.

He was damaged inside and out.

He was poor and she was rich.

He had nothing to offer her.

He had his one chance at happiness long ago and it was all taken away in a flame of destruction.

He was better off on his own.

It was a familiar litany of despair, often repeated, but the truth of the matter was unassailable.

In spite of every reason he could throw against it, he had serious feelings for this woman.

Deep, serious feelings that nothing in his litany of rational reasons could diminish in the least.

He cared for her.

He would love her if he could.

He was royally screwed.

As he had done so many times before, Andy Patterson turned off this vulnerable side of himself and concentrated on the business at hand.

Today. Astrid and Oscar. A win, if possible. Then, one more night and home.

He collected the dogs from Vilma and warned her they would be leaving in twenty-five minutes.

She was wearing a huge, white, hotel robe over a long filmy nightdress and looked sleepy and soft like a puppy or a small child. He hardened his heart and took the dogs for a fast run.

When he returned, she had dressed and ordered breakfast for both of them which he gulped down rapidly without really tasting it, but glad, nonetheless, for the calories to keep his energy high.

They were parked at the convention centre and in place for the competition in good time. Vilma went off to get a seat and he scanned the performance listing to see how long he would have to wait.

Fortunately, he was placed early because of the previous day's standings. He noted this competition excluded most of the small breeds and favoured mid to large dogs whose agility was more evident.

He had paid close attention to the mid-sized dogs yesterday and assessed their performances, but today was an entirely different thing requiring a huge amount of skill and strength that was available only in the best of animals under the best of training plans.

He could only hope and pray he had done enough to prepare Astrid and Oscar. He secured the dogs in a quiet corner and went out to walk the course. The first part was much as he expected. The challenges were of moderate difficulty. The second part of the course, which would be where only the best of the morning's participants would compete, was at another level altogether.

He examined the height of the obstacles, comparing them to the extension capabilities of his dogs' legs.

He walked the distance between the tunnel and the ramp. He stood and eyed the zigzag course and estimated the largest dogs would not be able to change direction as fast as required.

This alone gave him a modicum of hope. It was a far more difficult set up than he had ever encountered in his years of training King for police work.

He returned to Oscar and Astrid, who welcomed him eagerly. There were ready to go; bright eyed and bushy tailed. He brushed their gorgeous coats to soothe himself more than to make them look more appealing. He talked to them calmly although his heart was hammering in his chest.

They knew. Dogs always knew. They pushed up against him, one on either side and forced him to sit down. They sat and stared at him with tails waving. The message was clear.

They were here.

They were ready.

They would do whatever he asked of them.

He could ask no more.

Everything around him faded from view. He saw only the two dogs and the course. He had decided to do something risky and unusual. Because of the closeness of the two dogs and because they had been trained together, he intended to run the course simultaneously, with Astrid in the lead and Oscar following only a few seconds behind. The risk was that Oscar might not get the signals fast enough to maintain the required control. Astrid was smarter, faster and the leader. He was relying on her to get the instruction quickly and move on independently while he focussed on Oscar.

There was one part that might prove to be disastrous. In tunnel practises in the barn, Oscar had the habit of trying to catch up with Astrid and nip her tail before she could exit. The only way to prevent this, while the dogs were out of sight, was to delay Oscar's entry just long enough to give Astrid a head's start. The danger was that their emergence would be out of synch with their entry. The required standard was for the dogs to maintain an equal distance from each other all the way through the course.

The initial phase would show their mettle but the delay between the competitions in phases one and two was a concern. If the dogs were too wound up in the first phase they might lose their edge before the second and most important part.

There was not much he could do about this. Time would tell.

They were up and off soon after the announcements. All went well. Astrid went separately in this set with Oscar following as next competitor. He did not want to give away his master strategy too soon. Both dogs performed well and passed easily into the second phase.

Several animals were eliminated for faults but one beautiful, red, Hungarian Vizsla was an outstanding performer and drew an appreciative sigh from the audience. She would be the one to beat, but she had the long legs of her breed and there was a chance she would falter on the low tunnel task.

In the break between the two sets, he took the dogs out to a fenced area where they could run free. He had signalled to Vilma, who had a front seat, to join them outside. She left her coat on her seat and as soon as the dogs saw her emerge they swarmed her and she lavished them with praise and love in a way he admired, but could not reproduce. His police training did not allow such extravagant expressions of emotion with a working dog.

They loved her with their whole hearts. They trusted him and enjoyed their exercises as a way to demonstrate their strength and power. The two attitudes were complementary but quite different.

He thought, as he watched the trio laugh and play, that he and Vilma were also quite different. The question was; could they ever be complementary?

The few minutes of freedom were quickly gone when the warning bell sounded. It was back to business but the break had accomplished a fresh burst of energy in the dogs. He hoped it was enough.

He sat with Astrid and Oscar but did not permit them to see the arena performances of the first two competitors. The first dog, a good, slender young pointer, was too eager and knocked over a post.

Andy put it down to inexperience and nerves. The hall was now full to the brim and the excitement was palpable. He stroked his dogs and waited for the signal to begin.

The announcer said the next would be a challenging round, one of only three similar attempts they would see today.

As soon as the voice echo died down, he walked smartly to the starting point and stood ahead of the simple stair climb and jump with the dogs, one behind the other, waiting for his signal. Once they began, there would be no pause until they completed the course.

They were off!

Astrid was going fast, so Oscar had to match her speed. Andy stayed ahead of them and monitored the delays to keep them evenly spaced. It went by in a blur, so great was the required concentration, but when the tunnel appeared he changed tactic and stood at the tunnel entrance to keep Oscar back for a second more. Astrid vanished with a wave of her tail and Andy counted in his head. If he missed this calculation, his chance of a perfect score would disappear.

He hardly breathed as he walked briskly to the finish line. He turned, hoping to see Astrid emerge immediately but he was required to wait. The audience also waited in suspense. This was the final test.

Astrid burst out of the tunnel and exactly five seconds later a jubilant Oscar emerged and the two dogs ran to sit obediently at his feet, expecting the praise they knew they so richly deserved.

The arena erupted. Even the announcer was applauding. Vilma was on her feet, as were the judges.

It was a glorious moment, founded on endless hours of practice and the trust between man and dogs.

Andy withdrew and went outside at once. Their participation was finished. It would be an hour or more until the judges awarded their prizes. The parking area was silent and the enclosure was vacant.

To his surprise, he saw Vilma running toward him with her arms out, coat flying and purse dangling from her hand. She launched herself at him before he could summon his defences. His arms clenched around her automatically and her voice sounded in his ear with words he never thought to hear.

"Andrew Patterson, you wonderful man! That was a *tour de force!* You were amazing and everyone in there knew it. I can't believe how you handled these two monsters. I love them and I.............."

He was not about to let her finish just in case the sentence ended differently than he hoped.

He bent her over his arms and kissed her mouth soundly and often until the beat of their hearts was synchronized and the dogs lay down in shock at their feet.

CHAPTER 24

Vilma did not go back to her seat for the awards ceremony. Her mind and body were in a state of turmoil and she needed to think about what had happened. The problem was that her mind refused to cooperate. Her brain was not functioning at all it seemed. All she could remember was the exquisite feeling of being in his strong arms knowing he was present with her in a way he had never been before. It felt like stripping back a heavy drape and seeing out of a window for the first time. The view from that window was not yet clear but it was certainly compelling.

She stood in the foyer surrounded by tables and with the glass wall between her and the arena floor.

The announcements were piped in so she heard

the judge say Andy had won the Best in Brace and both the Agility and Obedience awards. Photographers were taking pictures of Andy with her dogs. She should be out there with a camera but that was a million miles from her mind.

She was reassembling everything in her life and it took all the mind power she could summon.

Andy Patterson and her?

A relationship?

A romance?

What and where?

When?

Now?

She was practical enough to realize they were far from home. Far from the view of anyone who might know them. If they were to take this 'thing', she did not yet have a suitable descriptor, to the next level, here and now, some kind of trial, was the obvious answer.

The obvious question was did she want to? The answer came in a flood of emotion that was overwhelming. Her body screamed, Yes! Yes! Yes!

She was almost embarrassed at this response and glad no one could see the flame in her face.

She calmed the turbulence within, by making a promise to herself….. *if* Andy still felt the same when they returned to the hotel, she would not hesitate.

It was a revolutionary decision, given her determined position of the years before. And yet, this could be her last chance for a fuller life. Not a life she could control in all respects. That would not happen with Andy Patterson. Not a life predictable and cozy. That was not in the cards.

Despite a series of negative reasons her brain was beginning to put in line for her, she stopped it short.

These matters were for the unknown future. Now was the time and place to find out if there would be a viable future for them.

The audience began to filter out of the building. She went to the car and waited.

It was a long time before Andy and the dogs arrived. Dusk was falling and the temperature was sinking fast.

She saw him approaching, his arms full of trophies and photographs, the dogs attached to him by leashes slung over his arms, but his eyes were only for her and her heart lifted at the sight.

They said little on the way back to the hotel. The dogs were already sleeping in the back seat. Without a word he parked the car, roused the dogs and took them inside to her suite where he settled them with premium chews and water bowls and lavish amounts of dry food. He then returned to fetch her and take her to his suite.

She let him be in charge. She knew there would be awkward moments but that was inevitable and temporary. She felt such admiration for this man, not only because of his accomplishments with her dogs, but also because he had chosen to make himself vulnerable; finally casting off the veneer of his tough exterior and letting her glimpse the tender depth that lay inside.

All of that was present but, in the end, it was the feeling of his arms around her that convinced her to let go completely.

His passionate words helped, of course.

They woke to a bright new day and a bright new future. Neither wanted breakfast but copious cups of coffee were enjoyed, after hot showers and fast packing.

Functioning as a pair for the first time and yet, knowing what each must do, they separated, with Vilma taking care of the bill and Andy looking after the dogs, much subdued after their efforts of the day before.

They set off early and there was a lot to talk about on the way to Kingston. Andy drove and Vilma looked at his profile and saw so much more there now that he had the look of a happy man. Predictably, the practical matters of what next, and where and when, were set aside for now. With his attention on the road and his eyes forward, he felt free to open up about his longing for connection, his admiration for her and his fear of never rising above the restrictions he had placed on his life.

"When you came into my life, Vilma, I was drawn to you immediately but I was afraid of rejection and not yet in a good place. Just knowing you would be arriving at the farm with the dogs gave me the will to think and act differently. My recovery is all about you. I know I never gave that away until yesterday. I know that was wrong. I know I can change. Now that I have you in my life, for real, everything changes."

He reached for her hand and squeezed it hard.

"I understand what comes next is up to you Vilma. I can't give you much because I don't have much other than myself to give, and I give that with my whole heart. Everything else is in your hands. You must decide and I do not want to rush you in any way. You must set the pace. You have so much more than I to lose."

She had listened carefully until this point. The flow of words comprised more than he had ever shared before on any topic. Now she had to interrupt.

"Andy, don't put me on some high pedestal. I am a woman who has had both joy and sorrow in my past. Not to the degree you have experienced, of course, but I am as surprised and shaken by what happened yesterday as you are. I had given up on finding a man I could love. I thought we had a business arrangement until you kissed me."

They both laughed, then they smiled, and Vilma reached up to touch the side of his face with tenderness and delight.

"So, you see, you are not the only one in a state of shock today. It's not about losses and gains and who has what. It's only about us. Us. Together."

She let that statement sit there in the car space for a moment. It was simple, but powerful, and said it all.

"We have time, Andy. Our feelings grew slowly, in silence. We have a lot of that silence to fill in and we will take the time we need to do it."

Without actually discussing it, the decision was made to make the journey home in one long drive. Vilma called ahead to alert Faith and they drove into Kingston to find her waiting outside the house with

Melvin, bag packed, and with a full carrier bag at her feet.

"Hi guys! Hi doggies! Hope you have space for this lot. Pauline and Mason have been very generous to me with early birthday presents. They want to talk to you, Vilma. Go on inside!

Andy, could Mel meet the dogs now?"

Vilma extricated herself from the car and stretched, pulling her clothes straight along with her facial expression. What had Faith got up to now?

The couple were alone in the family room and they started in at once.

"We know you are anxious to get home. We won't delay you. Pauline and I just want you to know we had a great time with Faith. She is so good with Mel, and the little ones love her like a big sister. Could you please convey this message to her Aunt Honor? We hope to see Faith again soon. We will call Honor to talk about how to do it but we feel it's important to keep up the contact."

Vilma breathed out. She had held her breath expecting trouble. This was good news. Today was golden. Nothing could spoil it.

She thanked Mason and Pauline and assured them she would be their advocate.

In mere minutes they were back on the road with

Vilma driving and Faith chattering on about all they had seen and done in two days.

"There's a lot to do In Kingston and it's so neat down by the water. You can take cruises and stuff to the islands. Mason wants to buy a small boat one day. Pauline has a brother with a boat and a cottage. They said I can go there next summer."

It was an hour on the way before she thought to ask about the dog show and Andy was glad to fill her in on this with frequent additions from Vilma's perspective.

Faith was impressed. She was also aware that the atmosphere in the car was utterly different from before. She could not quite identify the difference but she was sure something other than a big trophy win had happened near Cornwall, Ontario.

Once on the other side of Toronto and heading for London, they stopped for a break and a change of driver at a service centre.

The dogs had a run, Faith stocked up on food and she took the chance to ask Vilma a question.

"Okay. What gives? You two are not talking much but there's something going on."

"Uh, what do you mean?"

"Well, you let me burble on about school stuff all the way to Kingston but I could feel a tense atmosphere in the car. Now you let me burble on about Mel and the Jeffries' all the way home again, but the atmosphere now is electric between you. Did you guys have a giant fight or something?"

"Not exactly, Faith. Look, I need you to be very grown-up about this. Things have changed between Andy and me. We need time and space to work it out. Please say nothing to anyone yet."

"Sure, if that's what you want. I can keep a secret."

"Thank you."

Faith smiled, but it was a deceptive smile. She could promise all the promises Vilma Smith wanted.

Faith knew these two were not going to be able to conceal their changed feelings for long.

Just then, Andy came racing in from the parking lot with the dogs, saying icy rain had started and the road surface would get slippery very fast.

It was time to go.

The two hours it took to drive back to London were difficult. Andy drove in steady, pounding, icy rain with darkness descending. Faith comforted the dogs, who were alarmed by the sound of rain on the car roof. Vilma prayed they would arrive safely. She knew Andy must be as tired as she was and the sight of several vehicles sliding off the highway was not in any way comforting to her.

The rain eased on the outskirts of London and they picked up speed for a few miles then slowed again as they reached the icy country roads. Traffic was light. Everyone else was home and dry by now.

The light shining out from the top of the tower at Harmony House was the welcome sign they all longed for.

Faith ran for the house first, with backpack and presents bumping against her legs. Andy set out for the woods, ignoring the rain, as the dogs needed to be free to run for a few minutes. Vilma parked the car in the garage and collected their luggage. There was no way she was going to send Andy Patterson home to that desolate, cold and cheerless shack after a day like this one. There was a good chance the residents of Harmony House were tucked safely in their beds. She would invite Andy to her room for the night and let come what may the next morning.

She held a large umbrella over her head as she slowly struggled with the luggage along the slick path to the side of the house.

Andy arrived with the dogs a minute later. They were all three soaked to the skin and when the dogs shook off the rain, she also was drenched. It was too funny not to laugh at the sight.

Nothing even remotely romantic about this! thought Andy, as he contemplated the long drive back to the farmhouse in his truck, in the dark, alone.

Vilma did not ask; she acted. Faith had left the front door unlocked for them. She pulled Andy inside before he could protest, dried off the dogs' feet as usual, and then signalled him to follow her. He thought they were heading for a hot drink in the kitchen and stopped short when he realized that was not her destination.

"Wait!" he whispered. "I thought we were going to go slow on this?"

"Andy, dear man, I can't send you out into the cold again. There's plenty of room for two here and the dogs will settle down in their familiar cage. I'll hang your clothes up to dry and you can skip out early or brave the stares tomorrow. Whichever you wish, but tonight you will stay with me."

He did not need a second invitation. He stepped into Vilma's lavish, spacious, suite, with a sigh compounded of relief and delight. Now he would see how she lived. Now he would be a part of her memory in this very personal space.

It was more than he expected. It was faster than he imagined. But then, everything had happened very suddenly and they had wasted so much time already. From now on the pace would accelerate and tonight was only the start. By the morning, in familiar circumstances, the magical night in Cornwall would be tested in the clear uncompromising light of day.

He was more than ready for their life together to begin. Vilma was a strong woman. He was sure she could run the gauntlet of her friends' reactions with confidence and natural grace.

As for his reactions?

Andy Patterson knew he would never be any less than extremely proud to be by her side.

Any time.

Any where.

CHAPTER 25

Faith was as good as her word and had a very low-key sixteenth birthday at the end of November.

She had saved the presents from the Jeffries' family and insisted she needed nothing more. Honor gave her a seasonal clothing allowance inside a card which was a gift her niece especially appreciated.

Faith was determined to make it clear to her aunt that she had not been superseded by the 'new' family.

"It's kind of a novelty for me right now, Aunt Honor. It's as if I went back in time and had a normal family life for a while. It might not last. *You* are my real family."

This message was delivered with a supportive hug and Honor was content.

Jolene's mother held a Sweet Sixteen party at her house, in the finished basement which was large enough to contain the J.J. gang and several others who had joined up after Faith had become the talk of tenth grade for her outspoken campaign against drugs and a second one campaign called, 'Back off Bullies!'.

This was a new venture for her and another learning experience.

She had never personally had a problem with bullying. Her former schools and foster homes were the proving ground. She learned fast that giving in once to bully tactics was an invitation to endless demeaning behaviour. It started with rude comments about her dirty clothes or hair and commenced rapidly to pushing, stealing and beatings that were planned to show no bruises on any exposed skin.

By the time she was nine, she had a strategy in place. Never let it start. Finish it fast.

Soon her tough demeanour signalled to all comers that she was no pushover. She became immune to attack but she could spot an easy target within two days in a new school or foster placement and that was when she began to defend the weaker ones against the bullies. Often she was the one who was dragged to the principal's office, or social workers' department, for aggressive behaviour. The victim fled while Faith took the punishment.

It was all a part of her descent into rebel territory.

That was behind her now. Now she had a home with people who cared, extended family in Honor and the Jeffries, a school she liked to attend and friends who admired her guts. Standing up in front of the entire school and 'telling it like it was' had earned her respect, recognition amongst the vast throng of grades nine and ten, and more. For her sixteenth birthday, her teachers presented her with an award for Community Service. That was nice, but what was even more significant was the way she fell easily into this kind of work. An idea began to grow that she, Faith Joan Jeffries, could aspire to train for social work and make a difference in the lives of kids who, like she once was, were rejects of the system.

∽

By mid-December, Hilary and Mavis were scrambling to organize a Christmas celebration that seemed to be receding faster than they could chase it.

As soon as they settled on a guest list, another unexpected announcement arrived and changed their tentative plans.

"What are we doing wrong, Mavis?"

"Nothing at all! You must look at this as another measure of our success at Harmony House."

"How on earth do you reach that conclusion?"

Mavis poured her friend a third cup of tea and moved Marble off the sofa cushions so she could turn more easily to confront Hilary face-to-face.

"Think of it like this:

Jannice is going to the O'Connors' to renew acquaintance with the lovely young couple who live in her old home. Shortly after this she is off to Quebec City for an important meeting that may well affect her future.

Faith and Honor have accepted an invitation to the Jeffries' place in Kingston to experience a family Christmas with children, such as Faith has never known. They will stay in a hotel, a first for Faith.

Eve will be in St. Mary's at the Annual Christmas Market where her art will be on display.

You, Hilary Dempster, have been asked by your son Desmond to share his Christmas Day in his brand new apartment in a downtown highrise, which is something you ought to do.

Now I ask you, which of these amazing events

could possibly have occurred without the intervention of all of us here in this home?"

Hilary's eyebrows reached their zenith. She choked on her tea and by the time she had coughed, wiped her mouth and recovered, she had managed to absorb the lesson Mavis had delivered.

"Goodness! I do see what you are getting at. I was thinking in terms of negative results compared to last year's wonderful catered Christmas meal. All those lives you mentioned have expanded beyond belief despite some serious difficulties and demands."

"And don't forget Thanksgiving! That was a true symbol of all we have done right. The group around our table had expanded rather than contracted and it was a wonderful evening in all respects."

"Of course it was! I don't think we can expect two such evenings in the same year. That would be greedy.

So, Mavis, that leaves you, Vilma and Andy, I suppose. What will *you* do?"

"Ah! That brings up another unexpected development. Remember the torrential rains that started in early November and went on for weeks?"

"Absolutely! We were safe here on high ground but there was flooding in the Thames River valley, at

Fanshawe Lake and in other low-lying areas with resulting flooded basements and so on.

Why do you bring that up? I think most of the water damage has been fixed by now."

"Not completely."

It was Mavis's turn to delay. She sipped her tea, which had cooled over the minutes of their conversation, then launched into the disturbing part of her news.

"Vilma came to me the other day when you were doing your volunteer driving. It seems the rising water engulfed Andy's old farmhouse which was low-lying near a far-off branch of the Thames."

"Oh no! What about his barn where the training business is set to start?"

"Luckily, that was spared as it is on higher ground with a solid concrete base. Andy thought the house would survive but when the water receded, the damage was extensive. There was only a root cellar below the ground level and that filled with water and dislodged the weakened foundations until the walls began to crack and the house became unsafe for inhabitants.

Vilma tried to conceal her relief from me. You know she never liked the old farmhouse. She says Andy is camping out in the big barn for now but major decisions must be made soon."

"What bad news for them! Will there be any insurance money to help?"

"Vilma says there should be, eventually, but the company is overwhelmed with applications right now.

Andy has managed to hire a generator so he can cook and have some heat."

"That doesn't sound like much fun. Did Vilma suggest Andy moves in with her for now?"

"Not right away. He needs to keep an eye on his equipment. I said he will freeze when the real cold arrives and she replied he would not have a choice by then."

"So, you can count on those two being here for Christmas? It will be a very small celebration with just three of you."

"Maybe not."

"What next? Why am I the last one to hear about all this?"

"It isn't deliberate, Hilary. You have been busy and some of these plans just developed recently.

Louise and Dennis have asked me to join them on Christmas Day. When they heard what's been going on over here they were quick to include Vilma and Andy and they wondered if you and Desmond would join them for the evening, if not for the meal itself."

Hilary's eyebrows did another dance as she absorbed this news. She was secretly delighted to have an alternative to spending a whole day with her son. Their relationship was somewhat more comfortable since he settled in London, but she feared their conversation would run out after an hour or two and leave a large and obvious gap of silence.

"How kind! I will ask Desmond what he thinks. My feeling is he will accept. He has heard about Dennis and Louise and I believe he is curious about them."

"Right then! That's all settled. We will do the decorations as before, but we need not do much more than that this year. I am pleased at the way it has worked out. A quiet time will be welcome. Since the end of summer it has been frantic here with one thing or another."

~

Vilma had helped Andy to move the best of his belongings out of the old house before it completely collapsed. There was not much to save. Mostly it consisted of the bright red items she had donated for his comfort. The furniture, such as it was, was in poor shape to start with. Andy's bed had developed a broken leg on the first occasion when they had tried to share it for a night. The event led to much laughter and a search for books substantial enough to prop up the broken leg.

Vilma made a joke of the whole thing but she was confirmed in her belief that she could never live with Andy in the old house. It was a predicament, until the torrential rains solved the problem.

Temporarily.

The question of where they would live together had not yet been answered. Andy was willing to spend an occasional night at Harmony House although he was very much aware of the presence of so many other women nearby.

Vilma had to proceed carefully so as not to hurt his male pride. She could have provided enough money for a down-payment on a modest house somewhere, but that gesture would have undermined Andy and separated him from his only source of decent earnings with the future dog training business.

She was pinning her hopes on the insurance settlement. With that, and a matching contribution from her own funds, they would, hopefully, have enough to rebuild on a higher elevation, eradicating the old farmhouse and its dire memories and incorporating some of the home comforts she needed.

She thought they might get a grant to use solar technology on the roof to defray costs. The original well was still there to supply their water. London was expanding ever outward from the core and it might not be too long until they could be hooked up to city facilities.

As she made her preliminary plans, she realized there was something of true beauty in the location. The stream with the trees was a haven for wildlife. The higher ground would provide a new house with stunning views over farmland and woods. Andy could build a garden around the new house to help it blend into its surroundings. They could have a garage for her car and a dog run to keep the dogs away from the nearby farmer's goat herd. The location was certainly private and secluded. They could eventually expand into further premises for dog kennels. There was money to be made in supplying safe and healthy accommodations for animals while their owners went off on holidays.

At this point, she thought of something else entirely.

It was not a new thought. There had been a partial discussion along the lines of formalizing their relationship.

"Would you ever want to leave Harmony House and live with me? I will ask you to marry me, one day, Vilma. You know that."

The question was whispered while she dozed in his arms in the comfort of her big bed at home. There were two questions being posed, and she had no immediate answer for either of them. Breaking her contract at the house was an unknown, but presumably a possibility. It depended on how she really felt about making a break from the women to whom she had become as close as family.

Breaking her vow to never enter into marriage again was a different proposition entirely.

She adjusted the position of her head so as to look into his beautiful, deep-green eyes.

"Is marriage something you feel we need, Andy?"

"I am mostly concerned about what *you* may need. This is an uneven yoking in many respects and perhaps the formal arrangement would make it easier for you."

She laughed. "I don't care a whit what people think. I had two large, expensive weddings and neither one of them ensured perfect happiness for long. I don't need to do any of that again. How we feel about each other is a far better predictor of our success than all the trappings of a fancy ceremony."

He laughed again. "Good! I was not looking forward to that. My experience has been similar.

Please think about the future, my darling, and let me know what you want me to do so that we can be together for longer than one night at a time."

For Vilma, there was one way to accomplish this without too much delay. The February week in Jamaica was fast approaching. The island had escaped the worst of the tornadoes of the early part of the fall season.

She and Andy could go there as a couple and occupy one of the cottages. It would be like a proper honeymoon; something they really needed to cement their relationship.

She could rent out the remaining cottage and that would pay for their holiday. She had an idea to solve two problems in one by finding rental candidates from an unusual source; a source that would provide compatible occupants with much in common with Vilma.

She stopped abruptly.

She was constructing in her head, a vast and complex future for them without including Andy in these decisions. She must not do this. It was demoralizing for him to be presenting with a *fait accompli*.

She had years of planning for herself. She must not start out by putting him in an inferior position.

He had asked for her input. The discussion would start from that point and she would be careful to go slowly and resist overwhelming him with her extensive ideas. This was the way she must proceed in future if this relationship was to be successful.

CHAPTER 26

Mavis Montgomery was spending quite a lot of time with Louise Ridley now that her garden had been put to bed for the winter months. Louise found her to be a sympathetic and restful companion whose advice and help seemed to blend seamlessly with that of Hilary, who Louise considered her guardian angel.

Mavis became Louise's closest confidante shortly after they had a conversation about the social work Mavis had done while working at the courthouse.

"What happened to those families with severe drug or mental issues?"

"It depended on what resources were available for them in the city. Sometimes a foster family could be found to care for the children while a parent was undergoing help in a hospital facility. Sometimes, sadly, the family was never able to reform because the time apart was too long and older children moved to take up their own lives elsewhere."

"How sad for them!"

"Yes. Many of the stories ended badly."

Mavis was thinking about Faith and how close she was to being a lost child with no place to go.

Louise was thinking about small children who needed love and support while separated from a sick parent.

"How many of the cases you describe involved more than one child needing temporary homes?"

"Most of them, I'm afraid. By the time the situation was so advanced that the courts were involved, a family had grown, as did their problems of unemployment, or absent fathers."

"Were these children able to be housed together?"

"Only very rarely could that happen. Registered foster families usually had one or two youth or children already and the influx of three or four more was impossible to arrange. Of course it could be very destructive for the children to be separated when their family unit was already under stress. Many spent years trying to get back together again."

Louise appeared to be strongly affected by these

stories. Mavis began to wonder why she was so concerned.

"What makes you ask, Louise?"

"I am so sad for these children. I must confess to you, Mavis, that much of my mental distress was related to my inability to have a child. You see, I come from a large family. Life with children around was what my childhood was all about. As one of the oldest, I looked after my little brothers and sisters and loved it all. Mother called me 'her little helper'. I seriously thought of becoming a child nurse specializing in the care of babies, but my life took a different turn when I met Dennis and moved far away from my family home. I haven't been in touch with my siblings for years now."

She stopped talking, and Mavis could see how painful these memories were to her. With the new strategies she had gained from psychotherapy and from knowing there was help readily available next door, Louise could now pull herself back from the dangerous brink where failure could lead.

Mavis watched this recovery process happen right in front of her and she knew Louise was safe.

"What are you thinking about, Louise?" Mavis spoke in a gentle and tender voice.

The silence deepened and the ticking of the kitchen clock could be heard. It was the only sound in this large home. Mavis could relate Louise's story of her busy childhood life to the complete contrast of her life now. It was such a different and solitary existence. No wonder Louise had collapsed under the extreme disappointment of being childless.

Mavis went into problem-solving mode. She scoured her memory for a solution. She must move slowly and carefully. Louise's recent mental problems would not permit her to qualify for foster parent status but there was much that could prepare her and give her the comfort she desired without a formal qualification. That could come later. There was time.

"Louise, my dear, I am about to suggest something to you. Only you can decide if it is something you want. There is a program in London to train women for childcare responsibilities. You would work closely with qualified people and gain knowledge of how the system operates.

It would be a minor role for some time but you would be able to help vulnerable children and their families."

Louise Ridley turned her tear-filled eyes on Mavis with an expression that reminded the older woman of a cat she had once saved from drowning.

"Is this true? I would work like a slave for this chance. When could I start? What should I do to prepare? If I could eventually become a foster parent it would make me so happy and I'm sure Dennis would love to fill this house with the sounds of children's laughter. It was what we intended when we bought into the crescent. Oh, Mavis! Thank you for giving me hope."

There were tears to follow and noses to be wiped. Mavis was just as moved as was Louise, but part of her mind was still forming the plan.

Slow stages so as not to overwhelm Louise.

Get Dennis on board soon.

Look for a winter beginner course if possible.

Ask Faith to talk to the couple about some of her foster home experiences.

Bring Hilary into this. Louise would need a lot of support.

Several cups of tea later, and after a tour of the empty bedrooms with an exhilarated Louise who immediately had plans for decorating themes, Mavis set off back to Harmony House through the snow with visions of Louise surrounded with happy children in a house full of laughter.

Andy was surprised when Vilma suggested the February holiday in Jamaica. His first thought went to the expense. His second thought went to the dogs.

Vilma quickly assured him she had an idea to defray the cost but she needed some more time to put that in place.

"I have been thinking about the dogs, however. They would be most comfortable here at home. I am confident, Jannice and Faith, between them, could cope with the dogs' regular routines. Faith would stay with them overnight and we have time to coach both in the signals they respond to so well.

I will take Faith and Jannice for practise runs with the dogs in the woods if you clear some paths of snow for them. If they stick to the usual paths the dogs will do the rest.

It's only for one week."

Andy was beginning to grasp the ever-creative mind of Vilma Smith. It was a mind that never acknowledged an obstacle she could not surmount. He was somewhat less confident about the abilities of a woman and girl to succeed with two energetic dogs who had wills of their own.

"It's certainly an idea, Vilma. I suppose we have a few weeks to work on this but we should have a backup plan in case they can't cope."

"I am good with that, Andy. If you know of an alternative, I will be glad to hear of it."

She had deftly put the ball back in his court. He wondered if he would ever get used to this amazing woman who was so full of mental and physical resources.

The subject of the discrepancy in their ages had never come up. He knew why. She was his match in energy levels. She was his superior in emotional intelligence. She was creative and curious and positive and beautiful and......he could run on with this forever. Age had nothing to do with it. She was everything he wanted and needed, and he considered himself saved from a worthless existence and transported to heaven where he would happily worship at her feet. He would not allow himself to tell her this in actual words, however.

Vilma was nothing if not practical and his overtly romanticized statements were greeted with appropriate amounts of scepticism. She preferred actions to promises and he was delighted to provide these evidences of his affections whenever they were together and alone. Like now.

He looked over at the face he loved. He could deny her nothing. If she said there was a way, he knew she would find it and make it work for them.

They were a team. His part was to provide the strength and determination to match hers. He had all the incentive he would ever need, right here in his arms, to make this dog training centre a viable business. Until that was settled, he meant to continue gardening and snow-clearing with his regular clients and with the new city clients Hilary had been supplying for him. Now she was visiting older seniors regularly, she could see they needed more than driving help. Most wished to remain in their homes but had not the energy to do maintenance tasks like hedge and tree trimming. Hilary had reminded several of them that a poorly-maintained yard was an invitation to a break-in. Appointments for more garden work resulted from this.

He sighed deeply and thanked the gods for Harmony House and Vilma and Hilary and all the women.

He was certainly not unaware of the challenges ahead.

There might, in future months, be an occasional tussle with his Vilma over the plan to build a suitable house on the ridge overlooking the stream. He expected to have to rein in her decorating ambitions but before they reached that ultimate goal, the thought of a week relaxing together in endless sunshine in a beach cottage, sounded like exactly what would be needed. He could hardly wait to see his stunning Vilma in a bikini.

When Andy's truck was parked overnight near the garages, everyone at Harmony House knew he was staying with Vilma. There was an unspoken agreement to leave them in peace. Everyone knew their difficult situation with regard to accommodations and no one who had watched the slow development of their relationship was at all surprised at the outcome. The women conspired together to exit the kitchen early and leave copious amounts of bacon, pancakes and whatever else was available, in the warming oven for Andy's appetite. Vilma secretly gave Eve a meal subsidy to cover Andy's greater food requirements.

His presence was not a real problem as he always went off just after daylight to do driveway clearing jobs for people who lived at the city limits.

After Andy left Harmony House, happy and well-fed, Vilma mentally dusted off her hands.

Mission accomplished on the February holiday idea. The next part of her plan would require time and thought and not an inconsiderable amount of research.

For some time she had been wondering if Harmony House had similarly-successful models elsewhere in Canada. She thought there must be a group, or co-housing organization, where common problems and advanced ideas could be discussed for mutual benefit.

Online sources indicated there were over a dozen housing models ranging from small establishments like theirs, to almost full-sized apartment buildings. British Columbia had several and Saskatoon had an early version in a purpose-built condo complex called Wolf Willow. Alberta was one of the first provinces to adopt the co-housing model and they were about to begin a new multigenerational community based on the same principles.

This caught Vilma's interest. Since Faith joined the Harmony House community, she was forced to admit the girl had brought new life and energy to the other residents. Honor and Jannice were also proving to be valuable members in their different ways. The idea of mixed generations might well be the way forward for Harmony House. Faith would likely leave fairly soon. Goodness knows what Jannice would do now Mitchell Delaney had arrived on the scene.

She could only speculate on the advantages of a new approach to co-housing in a small facility such as theirs. Most of the ones she researched were much larger in scope and some even accommodated families. It was more like a village concept than an individual house for a few women.

She knew this might not be what Hilary and Mavis had visualized initially. It was not Vilma's job to tell them what to do in the future especially since she was most likely to be leaving Harmony House in the next year.

Something about the opportunity to take a winter break in Jamaica had started a line of thinking for Vilma. These women, and even some men, in co-housing communities spread out across the country, had much in common. Why couldn't they all band together and consider ideas to enlarge their options? Exchanging residences for brief periods of time could be beneficial for visiting distant family, medical needs, or simply for a change of scenery or a change of climate. The basic legal and financial requirements of their respective co-housing residences would remain in place. It would merely be a move to a different location for an agreed period of time.

A bit like AirBnB without the fear of an unknown person who might not respect the privileges.

Vilma thought such an organization should exist, if it did not already.

All the statistics suggested the population was aging rapidly. The projected rise in these numbers by the year 2036 was around 4.1 million.

A quick survey, locally, showed her there were

several new seniors' residences planned or started, but the monthly costs were always excessive and the investment uncertain.

For those who could afford to buy a share in a co-housing project, their future was much more in their own hands. They could recoup their investment whenever they wished.

She thought about these ideas and finally decided to send out letters or emails to a number of co-housing establishments she found online. She chose the smaller ones in hopes of finding a couple who might want to share the expenses of the second cottage in Jamaica. She enclosed photographs of the island location and information about her present situation in Harmony House.

It was a remote chance, but one worth attempting. If no one responded, she always had the option of asking the rental agent to find her a couple for the cottage. That option reduced the money she would receive by finding candidates on her own, but it also meant her idea of establishing connections with other co-housing proponents would need a different and more organized approach. With so much going on in her life at the moment, Vilma had to be content to let fate determine if this minor step was a viable way forward to a bigger future plan.

CHAPTER 27

Christmas Day dawned bright and beautiful. The evening before had been magical with the slow drift of fresh new snow covering the fir trees with festive white decoration. The bare branches of the forest trees were laced in white and there was not a sound to disturb the peace.

Andy and Vilma stood together looking out the window at Mavis's garden, now shrouded in its winter blanket.

Harmony House was even quieter than usual.

Jannice had left on Christmas Eve for her old house downtown.

Faith and Honor took the trains to Kingston two days ahead so they could explore the city from their hotel before going to join the Jeffries' family on Christmas Day.

Eve had arranged a ride to St. Mary's with a friend from the Byron Art Club, where she was now an active member. Their paintings had gone ahead and were displayed in a museum near the Christmas Market, but there would also be interactions between buyers and sellers at an open stall. It was an annual occasion, much enjoyed by art lovers. Eve was thrilled to be included. The participants would be entertained at a feast supplied by the town council in their handsome old building after the market closed.

Mavis was with Louise and Dennis helping with dinner preparations for three couples and thinking she could never have imagined this a year ago. Louise insisted Mavis was to be seated with the guests and not to hide away in the kitchen.

"We'll serve together and Dennis can carve the turkey and the roast beef. I expect you and Hilary to take any leftovers back with you, although how much will be left with three men to feed, is an unknown at this point!"

Mavis was delighted to see the confidence and sheer joy in the face of her neighbour who had advanced in leaps and bounds since her awful breakdown. Mavis could detect no signs of that now.

Her suggestion of a program to prepare Louise for a foster home application had given the woman a fresh ambition and she and Dennis were closer than ever in going forward with this plan.

Mavis's earlier footsteps across the lawn were all that could be seen from Vilma's window to break the snow covering on this special morning.

Vilma sighed contentedly.

"Let's go back to bed. I just heard Hilary moving along the hallway to the kitchen. We are practically all alone here for a change and there's no rush. The dogs will wait for a bit and I can make coffee right here whenever you want."

Andy was happy to oblige. Cuddling beneath the covers with Vilma and with two dogs as an extra heat source at his feet was a pleasure he could never get enough of.

Christmas Day.

He did not want to struggle to remember this time last year. It was a dark period in his mind only brightened by the thought of visits from Vilma and her dogs on the distant horizon.

How had everything changed so much in such a short time?

How had Vilma Smith managed to transform him in every way that counted?

How had he moved the million miles from his old farmhouse hideaway to this luxurious room in Harmony House?

How had he convinced this wonderful woman to accept his meagre existence and see it as a project to improve and enhance his life?

The truth was that he had resisted every attempt to brighten his surroundings, every move to get him to open up, every single opportunity to see her as more than the inept owner of two dogs.

She insisted, in their intimate moments, when truth was the only possible form of spoken communication, that she did not set out to draw him toward her.

"Exactly the opposite!" she confessed. "I was never willing to be pulled into the lifestyle you represented. I fought against it even while feeling grateful for your help with the dogs. I fought you with everything I could summon for many long months until I could deny my feelings no longer.

I believe if we had not been far from our usual haunts in that hotel, under such different circumstances, we might not have been able to break through our mutual barriers."

He objected immediately to this version of events. But it had the ring of truth about it. Vilma was not one to sugar-coat things in her life. His secret fears were based on the insecurity of that one moment in that one particular place where they came together for the first time. If his present immense happiness depended on that unusual conjunction of circumstances, it meant life and love were fragile, uncertain and ephemeral.

He turned in bed and looked at Vilma now sleeping soundly by his side with Astrid inching her way up the outer edge of the bed to rest against her owner's legs.

The realization struck him that this view of life and love was the only right one. Not a comfortable one, but valid nevertheless.

The conjunction of one moment in the wrong place had wrecked his previous life in a horror of noise and fire.

The outside chance of being employed at Harmony House at just the right time had brought him into the sphere of Vilma when she needed his help.

His wins at the dog show had impelled Vilma to open her arms to him, literally and metaphorically; an action he could not resist.

The unexpected rising water of the Thames River

had solved the serious problem of their future living accommodations.

Andy Patterson had to resolve this dilemma in his own mind. There was a lesson here. One he must figure out, then understand and accept, with gratitude in his heart.

He looked toward the window where the sun was shining on a fine day. He had no control over the weather. It was just one more of the elements around him over which he, and all others, had no control.

This was the underlying insecurity of life. So much was sheer happenstance; some with good results; some bad. The good was a gift. It must be seized with both hands and cherished; never questioned, and appreciated fully, each and every day, in the understanding that all could change in an instant.

This was the way forward for him and for Vilma. Every moment must be lived to the full. No regrets. No fears. Together against all the odds.

He placed a gentle kiss on her sleeping forehead and slid down into her warmth again.

It was Christmas Day. A day he knew he would never forget.

~

By New Year's Eve, Harmony House was back to its full complement of residents. It had been decided to welcome the new year with champagne toasts at midnight for those who wished to participate.

To Hilary's surprise everyone was in attendance in the winter dining room with glasses raised as the New York glitter ball on television dropped down to the usual wild acclaim.

She detected an air of excitement that was in addition to the clinking of champagne glasses and the good wishes exchanged for the coming year. It was not long before the television was shut off and she found out what had caused the suppressed feelings. The news announcements began at once.

"Before everyone goes off to bed, I want to tell you all about Quebec City."

Jannice O'Connor was lit up like a candle and her audience knew this was something different from her earlier account of the charming day with the O'Connor siblings in her former home.

"Of course I adored the ancient city and Mitchell was a wonderful host. We met in his home study to talk about my Irish heritage. He loved the photographs of the wedding trousseau and asked about every outfit. He wants to visit Eldon House and Museum London in the spring, but just today I got a letter from him telling me his proposal for a book has been accepted by his publisher and we will have to arrange many more sessions. Old tales brought to Canada are a major feature of his work. He wants *me* to be co-author! Isn't it exciting!"

There was no denying it. Her enthusiasm was infectious and congratulations went the rounds.

When the excitement died down a little, Faith had a chance to interrupt.

"Since we are sharing successes, I want you all to know I have passed my Shakespeare course."

Hilary led the cheers at this juncture.

"...........and also, still on the good news front, there will be an article in the local newspaper this month about my talks to students about good choices. They are calling me a 'Youth Ambassador' if you can believe it? Me, Faith Joan Jeffries, the despair of teachers everywhere! Before now, that is!"

Honor came to stand by her side and beamed with pride. She had been so pleased to see Faith's behaviour with the younger Jeffries' boys in Kingston. Honor and Mason had many good talks together about the early days with Felicity while Faith entertained the children. He insisted he could see similarities between the twin sisters. He stated Honor was the person Felicity should have been if her life had gone differently. Honor found something deeply comforting in his words. It felt as if an old wound had healed inside her.

She and Faith had hours of good conversation on the train trips to Kingston and back again. A new understanding was in place between them. They discussed the future and where that might lead Faith.

Her aunt almost wept when Faith acknowledged her debt of gratitude to the person who had taken her in even when she was 'totally obnoxious' to her.

Honor knew she now had an ally in Pauline Jeffries who told her the few days they had spent together had finally put to rest her husband's regrets and fears about his choices long ago. She invited Faith and Honor to stay in the summer when many more outdoor activities were available.

"My boys have really taken to your Faith. She seems to talk to them like grown-ups, not little kiddies, and they love it. She expects them to act like grown-ups too, which is a great relief for me, I can tell you. Melvin in particular, has grown by leaps and bounds since he met Faith. He calls her his 'big sister.'"

She and Pauline parted as friends and extended family members. Honor was delighted to feel she was no longer alone in her responsibilities to Faith.

Vilma observed how close together Honor and Faith stood during the announcements, and she knew what a good sign it was. The girl had finally proved her worth despite some poor decisions along the way. She felt more comfortable with her idea to leave Astrid and Oscar in her care in February.

The initial hand-over attempt was going quite well. She allowed Faith to supervise the dogs' morning walk, during the school holidays, while watching them like hawks from the house. No incidents had occurred so far.

With the current air of excitement in the room, Vilma wondered if she should announce the successful connection she had made through her extensive contacts with other Canadian cohousing projects.

A few couples of had responded positively and initial discussions were underway for the week in Jamaica.

Vilma had not yet fully broached this subject with Hilary and Mavis so she decided to delay until she received their blessing. The entire holiday/honeymoon week was in limbo until the insurance was settled on Andy's farmhouse replacement. That little job would be keeping both of them occupied for some months. The long term implications of the house reconstruction, was another conversation she needed to have with Hilary and Mavis. If all went well, Vilma would require her investment money from Harmony House. She would move to the new home with Andy, leaving a gap to be filled by another candidate.

Eve stepped forward as glasses were filled once more.

"My dear Harmony House family, I want to tell you I have sold five paintings at St. Mary's Christmas Market. The money will fund many more paints and canvases and a large tarpaulin to protect my carpet!"

Everyone laughed in sympathy and smiled to hear about her success.

"I have already been invited to participate in summer shows in Ontario, and I mean to accept. The art community has been very welcoming to me."

"Well done, Eve! This is brilliant news! I believe we will have to adjust your Kitchen Queen title to include Artist in Residence."

More cheering resulted from this *bon mot* of Mavis's but the party soon began to break up after everyone looked around the circle to see if more surprises were forthcoming.

In a few minutes, Mavis and Hilary were the only

two left. They had shooed all the women off to bed and were finished collecting crystal glasses on a tray for handwashing, and tidying up the dining room.

New Year's Day brunch was to be a casual affair in the kitchen with self-service.

"Mavis, come and sit here by the fire for a minute before we go off to bed."

Mavis looked up from brushing crumbs into a plastic bin and went to join her friend on the couch.

"What's up, Hilary? You must be tired by now. I certainly am."

"Oh, yes! But it's been such an ending to the year I feel we need to talk it over while it's fresh in my mind. Things around here have changed, Mavis, and they will be changing even more, if I'm not mistaken."

Mavis joined her friend on the couch with a sigh of contentment at being off her feet. The week between Christmas and New Year was such a busy one with gatherings of various kinds. She was glad January would bring her annual, self-imposed diet program, so she could lose the weight the festive season always encouraged.

"I do know what you mean. I looked around the group tonight and thought it might be the last time we seven would be celebrating together like this."

"Really? I was thinking along those lines myself,

but changes coming so abruptly? I thought we had more time."

"Well, I could be wrong. And yet, the future is rushing toward us."

"Isn't that a suitable prediction in the first hours of a new year! Are you feeling particularly prescient?"

"Not really, Hilary! I'm more weary than anything else.

The indicators are there to see, however, and can't be denied for long.

In two years Faith will be gone to higher education and she may be heading to Kingston for that, and possibly taking Honor with her. Honor can do her work from anywhere, after all.

Eve's horizons are opening up. Jannice will need time in Quebec. Vilma is building a new home and new life with Andy. I will be involved with Louise's ambition to foster children and you have a new interest in volunteering which you are developing into a major program, as I knew you would."

"*Goodness me!* When you put it like that it seems our cozy little family can't wait to depart from Harmony House. You and I are the only ones who may be fully based here. Have we failed somehow? Our original co-housing plan was for the long term, or so I believed."

Mavis shifted in her seat. She had not intended to depress Hilary with all these predictions. She must turn the negative into a positive, which was always her role in their friendship.

"Don't be too concerned, my dear. It depends on how you look at it. We two are the cornerstone.

If others decide to move on it has to be seen as success, not failure. We have managed to create such a warm and nurturing atmosphere in this lovely home that our little lambs, brought in from the storm, have grown and developed to their full potential under our care.

It's not a bad thing to nurture others as we have done. It's a great privilege. Perhaps new residents will fill the empty spaces here and new adventures will begin?"

"That is a lot to take in at this early hour, Mavis. I will need sleep before I can share your optimism.

Can you promise me at least a few months of comparative peace and quiet?"

Mavis smiled. She would promise, for Hilary's mental comfort, but the future was never totally knowable. The past few months in Harmony House proved that to be the case.

It could well be that the pace of change was just moving up another gear and both she and Hilary had better be prepared.

AFTERWORD

Ruth Hay's fourth series, **Home Sweet Home**, follows the ups and downs of six women attempting to live together for mutual support and safety.

The fourth book, titled, *Affinity House,* will be published in 2018.

Read Ruth's other series, *Prime Time, Seafarers,* and *Seven Days* on Amazon, Barnes & Noble, Kobo, and iBooks.

Also read Borderlines a stand-alone thriller.

www.ruthhay.com

Seven Days Series

Seven Days There

Seven Days Back

Seven Days Beyond

Seven Days Away

Seven Days Horizons

Seven Days Destinations

Borderlines (Standalone)

Borderlines

Home Sweet Home Series

Harmony House

Fantasy House

Remedy House

Affinity House (2018)

Printed in Poland
by Amazon Fulfillment
Poland Sp. z o.o., Wrocław